All She Wants

What Reviewers Say About Larkin Rose's Work

Breaking the Rules

"This is one hot steamy, raw, sexy and erotic romance. This is not a Princess Charming and her damsel in distress kind of story. These characters are way too strong-willed and opinionated for that. The story is bold, straightforward, and a good read." —*Rainbow Reflections*

Visions

"Past intertwines with present in Rose's (*Kiss the Rain*) charming new erotic romance. Fortunately, the seduction unfolds with enough spice and sweetness to keep readers satisfied." —*Publishers Weekly*

"I howled, applauded, panted, and dabbed away the tears from pure pleasure while reading this book. This is a wonderful multi-layered love story, peppered with nearly devastating confusion, and practically undermined by misunderstood class collision. I think it would be divine to see this as a play or movie, but the remarkably pure sexual heat would definitely limit the distribution venue. What a shame. At least there is the written word and that has masterfully unraveled the intimacy and details allowing me to savor the humor, the women, and the monumental obstacles seeking to crumble the wishes and desires for the star-crossed characters. I unquestionably recommend this!"—*Rainbow Book Reviews*

Kiss the Rain

"In this story Larkin Rose has created two awesome leading women who in their own way tower over everyone. I was truly dazed at the beginning and continued to be astounded throughout the novel. …I can, without a doubt, recommend this book for the extraordinary strength and stunning depth that each noteworthy woman presented to me over and over again. Transcendent! [The conclusion] sent me soaring and believing in miracles. This book is like ambrosia and a nearly perfect kiss among Eve, Jodi, and the rain. Incredibly satisfying!"—*Rainbow Book Reviews*

"Even if you're not a fan of erotica, Larkin Rose is an expert at knowing how to keep you turning the pages. *Kiss the Rain* is the story of what happens when Jodi and Eve meet during London's Fashion Week. It also tells how lives can change in seven days. The sex is extremely hot, and the tension is high. This is an enjoyable read which is perfect for a beautiful spring day." —*Just About Write*

Vapor

"This story possibly takes the ultimate award in having two people completely misconstrue each other. Plus, they never talk about it. Of course, with the super sizzling action between the sheets, on the staircase, in the washroom, who really has time to discuss anything? Brilliant, engaging, funny, tearful, and loaded with love, I was beguiled from the very beginning. Hats off to Larkin Rose, another Bold Strokes Books author, for masterminding this marvelous book."—*Rainbow Book Reviews*

No Leavin' Love

"This story feels like an allegory and from that viewpoint it soars, dips, spins wildly around its central theme, and certainly touched my own heart's periodic desire and longing to go home. These are two powerfully impressive women, who pretty much met their match between them. I certainly recommend you stay the course, enjoy the wedding, and then discover when or how the loose ends get resolved. Marvelously pleasurable!"—*Rainbow Book Reviews*

I Dare You

"Oh my goodness. Well, this is quite a lovely leap and a jump from Ms. Rose's first book. Gritty, sexy as all get-out, and broadcasting her leading women's passions, doubts, and strengths all over the place. I wouldn't want it any other way. Kelsey and Jordan are very strong characters and it is hard to imagine them not burning each other out or obliterating each other from the face of the earth. I found this pairing incredibly refreshing and provocative."—*Rainbow Book Reviews*

"Rose's well-crafted debut novel is erotica with benefits—plausible plotting, a fast pace, and well-defined secondary characters, including an engaging gay drag queen whose sturdy shoulder is always there when Kelsey needs grounded queer advice."—*Q Syndicate*

Visit us at www.boldstrokesbooks.com

By the Author

I Dare You

No Leavin' Love

The Pleasure Planner

Vapor

Kiss the Rain

Visions

Breaking the Rules

Dangerous Curves

All She Wants

All She Wants

by

Larkin Rose

2019

ALL SHE WANTS

ISBN 13: 978-1-63555-476-2

This Trade Paperback Original Is Published By
Bold Strokes Books, Inc.
P.O. Box 249
Valley Falls, NY 12185

First Edition: September 2019

Credits
Editor: Cindy Cresap
Production Design: Susan Ramundo
Cover Design By Tammy Seidick

Dedication

To Cindy, the coolest editor an author could ever have. That whip of yours, well, I kind of like it! *grin*

To Rad, because without her, BSB wouldn't even exist. Thank you!

To the readers, as always, every word on these pages is for you.

And to Rose…another book, another year, and you are still the love of my life.

Chapter One

Tessa Dalton slid the client's paperwork into a folder then dropped it into the filing cabinet and closed the drawer, eager to end her day of prepping for the upcoming wedding, the one for which she wouldn't be present. She stood and shrugged on her jacket, hoping, yet not hoping, she could sneak past her sister Michelle on her way out the front door.

If she saw Michelle again before she left, she would give Tessa those blue puppy dog eyes, roll out her bottom lip, hang her head, and walk away without a word, continuing her almost perfect attempt to make Tessa feel guilty about leaving the company even though she was entering a contest that could change her life forever. God knew she was going to miss Michelle, helping her plan dream weddings and being part of a family team. But finding her own path in this thing called life was her ultimate goal. Going after her own future, her own dream of being a well-known wedding planner, maybe even owning a venue of her own, was the only thing she truly wanted. Not continuing to make Michelle's dreams a reality.

Nor was it like she was leaving Michelle high and dry. Even if she did come out the other side of this eight-week adventure victorious, which she most certainly planned on doing, Michelle's business was booming, clients lined up for many months for weddings, and the calendar was full of upcoming events. Michelle would be more than okay without her. She'd made sure of it. So no. Tessa had nothing to feel guilty about.

More than anything, she wanted her sister to continue her success. And as much fun as Tessa had helping her along every step of the way, she wanted something different for her own life. Yet something identical. In a different setting. In a whole new state.

A new life was waiting for her out there. In the mountains of Colorado. This contest was going to open that door for her, and fulfill another dream of hers, to one day live there, whether she conquered this quest or not. She was going to step through these next phases like a damn boss and dare anyone to stand in her way.

Tessa grabbed her purse and took a final glance around the office. There was a huge chance that she would never work here again. A chance that she wouldn't have her sister in the office next door. Wouldn't have their assistants to eat lunch with or help plan those fabulous weddings with.

In just a few weeks, this life could be over for her and a new one beginning.

The thought made her smile.

"Did you really think you were going to sneak past me today? Of all days?" Michelle leaned against the doorframe, thankfully, with her red tinged lips in place and not poked out like a pouting toddler.

"Just getting everything squared away for you." Tessa pushed the chair under the desk and faced Michelle, wishing her older sister was more like their half sister, Monty, who couldn't wait to drop Tessa off at the airport, eagerly pushing her to go grab the stars, beyond thrilled that Tessa was going to hang her hat on the moon. And if she made it to the final week, when only two teams were standing, she was going to join Tessa in Colorado and do just that. Help her hang her hat on the moon.

"I know I've given you shit the past few weeks about leaving me, because I'm going to miss the hell out of my sidekick, my admitted favorite sister, but you know I'm proud of you, right?" Michelle curled her lip out and angled her head to the side, spilling her blond hair over a shoulder. "I'm so, so proud of you."

Tessa went to her and wrapped her in a tight hug. "I do know that. And I love you for it. And I'm really going to miss you, too." She stepped out of her hug. "Speaking of sisters, Monty asked me to relay a message. She said to bite her."

"The jerk." Michelle chuckled. "And let me guess. You're rushing out to meet her at that disgusting little bar where her disgusting twats gather to catch a glimpse of her. Or should we call it her favorite pickup fuck palace?"

"Be nice."

Michelle had never bonded with their much younger half sister. She secretly blamed the "other" woman, Monty's mother, for their parents' breakup. As much as Tessa loved and adored their father, the blame rested solely on his shoulders. He was the married one. He was the one with a wife and children waiting for him at home. He was the one who was supposed to be loyal and true. Having an affair had been his choice and his choice alone.

The hostility Michelle carried after that affair had trickled down to Monty, the innocent result of their father's mistake. The fling that rocked the sturdy ground beneath the Dalton family's feet. Their parents had tried to salvage the marriage, to no avail. Truth was, that attempt was nothing more than a Hail Mary pass. Their relationship had been doomed long before their father admitted his guilt, or he wouldn't have succumbed to weakness in the first place. Many moons before he hesitantly announced that he was going to be a father, again.

Tessa had remained neutral through the whole ordeal. No matter how sad she'd been, no matter how enraged she'd felt, she still loved her daddy. Even at only thirteen, she knew she had to continue to share that love between both her mother and her father. Actually, their mother had encouraged as much. She'd done the exact thing any mother should want for her children and did everything in her power to make sure they remained bonded to their father. But Michelle had refused to even speak to him. She wouldn't take his calls. Wouldn't answer his texts. And didn't lay eyes on the baby until Monty's first birthday. Even that was awkward, with Michelle standing in the distance, blank facial expression. But she'd gone, reluctantly and extremely verbal about her dislike of being made to go, but her appearance was a tiny step in the right direction and that was all Tessa could ask for.

Monty had been a happy, curious little thing, sharing Tessa's and their father's striking green eyes. She always wanted Tessa with her. Her love for Tessa kept her close, and their bond only grew stronger over the years.

While Tessa took pride in having another sister, Michelle refused to have any part of her. Even to this day, years away from that drama, her relationship was rocky with their father, and practically nonexistent with Monty except to exchange playful insults, and occasionally Monty would steal a hug. Their father had eventually married Monty's mother, and although their mother had come to grips with the outcome of her marriage, that it was over, that he had moved on, that she would do the same, Michelle just couldn't find the same peaceful conclusion.

Tessa doubted she ever would.

Michelle shrugged. "Like father, like daughter. Neither knows how to keep their dick in their pants."

Tessa couldn't argue with that. Monty had gained a reputation for being the town playboy. She dated no one, but fucked anyone. Married or single. Green, brown, black, or white. Monty had no partiality to the women she carried to her bed. A fact that drove Tessa insane. Color and creed were unimportant to Tessa as well. But that married thing. Absolutely not.

Monty was the opposite of the Dalton girls, or rather, the original Dalton girls, who were loyal, devoted, and were fairly picky when it came to relationships.

But Tessa couldn't love Monty more even if she hated that one ugly trait. That she was basically a slut who never asked questions because the answers mattered not.

"Hug me again, mean ass. I promised Monty I would meet her for a celebratory drink." Tessa squeezed Michelle as she stepped into her arms. "I'll update you every week, every day, and every chance I get. I promise."

Michelle faked a sniffle. "I want you to go rip all their heads off. Show them who the hell runs Colorado."

Tessa giggled. "I was taught by the best so they don't stand a chance."

Thirty minutes later, Tessa walked into the bar. Monty's second home. Hopefully, she wouldn't have to run off the eager beavers looking to be Monty's arm candy tonight. She wanted to spend some time with her without having to swat blatant invitations away.

This was a world she didn't understand. The women. She just couldn't understand them. It was like Monty had some magic aura around her that drew women, all women, married or not, right into her web. It was disturbing, actually. They just moved toward her, drawn to her perfect smile, hypnotized by Monty's daunting eyes.

It was sick. Especially the married ones. They made Tessa's blood boil. And sometimes, a lot of times, so did Monty.

As expected, she found Monty at one of the high-top tables, wearing her normal jeans and T-shirt, ball cap turned backward, and a group of women forming a semicircle around her.

Tessa sighed and made her way across the room. Without apologies, she eased onto a stool and took Monty's drink from her hand. "Sorry to interrupt your 'eeny, meeny, miny, moe' decision-making moment, but I only have a few hours to spend with you and I absolutely refuse to spend that time watching grown women beg to be the notch on your bedpost." She cut her sights on the women and let her gaze walk over each of their faces. "In case none of you understand my sarcastic comment, what that means is you'll have to come back later."

Grown, beautiful women. Well dressed. Appeared to have their shit together. Yet the fact that they were circling Monty like vultures proved they didn't. Whatever was wrong with them? Didn't they have self-respect? Didn't they care about love? Didn't they know that they were jostling for the attention of a well used fucking machine?

Yes. That was her sister. Monty. A fucking machine. And she was damn proud of it sometimes. She didn't care if she broke hearts. She didn't care if she busted up marriages. She just didn't care.

That part ate at Tessa the most. That Monty didn't care. That she could lay her head on her pillow every night and sleep like a baby knowing she'd slept with a married woman and that woman was going to go home to her wife and act like she hadn't just fucked a stranger. Nothing really mattered to her. She was out for one person and that person was herself.

God help her, but Tessa loved her anyway. No matter what. She had from the second her daddy carried Tessa to the hospital to meet the brand new tiny addition to their family. Tiny little fingers. Tiny little toes. Cute little button nose. And a head full of black hair. She was the cutest thing Tessa had ever laid eyes on, and she vowed to always be her friend and protector.

Problem was, she couldn't seem to protect Monty from herself. Especially when Monty didn't see anything wrong with the way she lived her life. With the many bar fights that had ensued from her careless behavior.

"Sorry, ladies." Monty gave each of them a sexy smile. "My sister appears to be a little grouchy tonight. Can we catch up later?"

The women gave sweet smiles to Monty then cut fuck you glares on Tessa as they slowly moved away.

Tessa gave a few finger waves as they, one by one, turned around and started across the room.

She looked back to Monty. "Don't you care that none of these women have any morals?" she asked as Monty looked away from their retreating asses.

"Morals? Who needs morals when you look that fine?" She took her drink back from Tessa. "Now, you have my undivided attention. Happy now?"

"Happy that I had to peel a huge portion of cheating women off of you? Not really."

"You ready to get this show on the road? Ready to go kick some ass?"

Changing the subject was Monty's cue that she was already over the motherly conversation. Sucked that Tessa always felt the need to be the mother figure. Why couldn't Monty just be a normal sister? Hanging out or shopping or even taking vacations together instead of this constant need to score? The life she lived, accumulating fucks, was far from normal.

JP, the bartender, set a beer down for Tessa with a wink. "Good luck with the contest, Tess. Go knock them all dead."

"Thank you. That's definitely my plan."

JP inspected Monty's drink then walked away.

"I haven't been nervous until now." Tessa took a sip, giving Monty the change of subject she seemed eager for. Fact was, she didn't want to talk about those women. She wanted to talk about her new adventure. She wanted Monty to calm her nerves in that natural way she had of easing Tessa's stress. "Michelle got all serious on me before I left tonight. Told me to go win the damn thing."

"Finally, she offers something intelligent." Monty set her drink down and slowly stirred the ice cubes. "Think she's ever going to like me?"

Tessa wanted to lie. She wanted to give Monty a shred of hope that one day her big sister would come to her senses and welcome Monty with open arms. Truth was, Tessa and Monty never lied to each other, no matter how ugly the truth was. That's likely why they got along so well. There was never any bullshit between them.

"Not a chance."

"Her loss. I'm kind of awesome." Monty picked up her drink. "Okay, so tell me how this contest works. Again."

Tessa angled her head, unsure if Monty was playing or not. "You're kidding, right?"

"Eight groups of five. I remember that part." Monty wiggled her brow playfully. "Oh, and you're the kickass leader of one of those groups."

"Yes. And? What else?"

"You get a secret client every week and you have to be their personal 'bend over and fuck me' workhorse."

"Just know that in eight weeks, if I'm still standing, after knocking out six other teams, you will be booking a flight to Colorado if only to come hold my hand. I'll be in meltdown mode at that point and running on pumped adrenaline."

"You think you're the shit? Think you can knock out all those other amazing planners? Think you got what it takes, Tessa Dalton?" Monty growled out her last question.

"Damn right!"

"That's my girl." Monty shucked her chin. "Send them all home in tears."

"Did you just change the subject because you can't remember the rest?" Tessa asked.

"What? Would I do that?" Monty pushed the glass to her lips.

"You can't remember, can you?" Tessa picked up a peanut from the basket and threw it at her. "You're an impossible jackass."

Monty dodged the flying food and laughed. "So violent! Fine. Fine. It goes something like this. You'll have an assistant planner, a decorator, a photographer, and a caterer, all at your disposal, all of whom already have experience working in their respective fields, and together you guys will plan whatever your secret client wants, like good little private escorts."

Tessa threw another peanut at her and again, Monty dodged to the side before she continued her description, almost word for word the way Tessa had described the contest.

"You won't know who your clients are until each Monday morning, unless you win top points, which you will because my sister is badass, in which case, you'll get their video, I think you said, on Sunday which gives you an extra day to plan, and then you'll have the week to strategize and put those plans into motion. Clients arrive on Fridays. You guys will cater to their every whimper and cry and all the blah blah blah in between until they leave on Sunday but not before they score each of your crew members in several different categories, each category changing every week to keep it fair, which is how the points are accumulated and a winner revealed. And if you score enough points, or rather, if you're not on the bottom, which you won't be, because again, my sister is badass, all teams except the losers get a night out on the town to be party animals. And to conclude, one team goes home each week until the final round, which is where I'll join you for all that handholding before your last hoorah, which will be an over-the-top extravaganza of a wedding, which you swear you hate, for whatever reason, even though you throw yourself headfirst into every detail of every wedding you've ever planned." Monty arched an eyebrow. "Did I get it right?"

"I think I'm going to throw up." Tessa gave her a smirk, but the truth was she was so ready to get this journey started. Beyond ready to get on with the next phase of her life.

And if all else failed and she didn't win, she wasn't out of the race. She was going after that new life, and even being beat out of a contest wouldn't stop her. This was just the beginning of reaching that goal. And she was going to do it in that breathtaking state. A place she'd been longing to return to since her first trip there.

A woman hesitantly walked toward the table and smiled down at Monty. "Hi. Do you remember me? I'm Abigail?" She pushed her straight hair behind an ear.

"Of course I remember. How could I forget you, Abigail? How have you been?" Monty smoothly took a sip of her drink, her brow creasing. Clearly, she didn't have a clue who this woman was.

Had Monty fucked so many women that she couldn't even remember their faces anymore?

The woman reached out for the chair closest to Monty as if the question was an invitation to have a seat. A diamond eternity band glistened on her ring finger.

The insinuation that she was free to have a seat, as well as that little band around her finger, pissed Tessa off quickly. What the hell was wrong with these damn women?

"No, sweetheart. No one gave you permission to join us." Tessa growled. She pointed toward the corner where the rest of the women had gathered. "You'll have to go wait with the other misfits until I am done with my sister." She leaned toward the woman. "But a word of advice. You should go right on back home to your wife. Tell her what a piece of shit you are for chasing after a piece of ass. And that you want a divorce. Be a fucking woman instead of a disgusting cheater."

The woman's eyes widened and she stepped back from the chair as if burned, her gaze immediately swinging to Monty then back to Tessa. "Me and my wife are—"

"Separated. Sure you are." Tessa sternly pointed. "Please go away from me. And don't come near this table again until I'm long gone."

Monty reached out for Abigail's hand and gave a gentle squeeze. "Please forgive my sister. Her delivery is crash and burn style." She pulled Abigail down and whispered in her ear.

Tessa rolled her eyes and slammed back in the chair.

Monty was incorrigible. She was downright disgusting.

The smile on Abigail's face was even more disturbing as she stood, gave Tessa a sorrowful expression, then scurried toward the bar, alone.

"What is wrong with you? Did our dad not give you enough kisses when you were little?" Tessa dove into big sister mode, the same mode that Monty claimed was mothering and smothering. She wished there was something she could say, something she could do, to make Monty see that her life was twisted. That this wasn't normal. That this was downright wrong on so many levels.

"God, don't start again, Tess. I'm single. I don't have to answer to anyone. And it's my life. Mine." Monty spat the final word, giving more impact to its meaning than she probably intended.

Fact was, Monty was her best friend. Her little sister. Her blood. There wasn't a single thing she could do to make Tessa ever disown her. To make Tessa hate her. But Tessa didn't have to like it, or even like her, and she damn sure didn't have to be quiet about it. Nor would she.

Tessa rose from the table, too angry to hang out any more, not to mention the next interruption she got from some bitch wearing a wedding band begging for another bitch to jump in her pants, was going to send her into full postal mode and it wasn't going to be pretty when she was done with the whole lot of them.

"I'm out, Monty." Tessa shoved the stool into place.

"No, Tess. Please don't go." Monty grabbed her arm and batted those puppy dog eyes. "I wanted to hear more about this contest."

Tessa pried her fingers loose, then kissed the back of Monty's hand. "I love you, dear sister, but I'm not in the mood for your rotten antics tonight. I have to get packed up, grab some sleep, then head to the airport first thing in the morning."

"I thought I was taking you to the airport."

Tessa glanced toward the corner. The women were glancing in their direction while they attempted to appear like they weren't.

Monty would be fucking one of them, possibly more than one, before long. Tessa was only standing in her way. God forbid she take just one night off. Michelle was right. Maybe Monty was a hopeless cause.

"I changed my mind."

"You don't trust me, do you?" Monty grinned, but Tessa could see the plea in her eyes. She didn't like it when Tessa was upset with her. Although she did very little to reverse the situation until she was done doing whatever Monty wanted to do.

"I trust you with my life." Tessa kissed the top of her head. "But I don't trust you to get me to that airport on time." She added a chuckle but didn't mean it. It wouldn't be the first time Monty had bailed on a plan. This time, that plan mattered more than anything. This time, the plan couldn't include her sister's crap or tardiness. "So, go put one of those idiots out of their wet misery. I'm going home to finish packing."

Tessa had been packed for weeks now. Monty knew that. But she didn't argue as Tessa walked away. Even she knew when Tessa had reached her limit. That limit was now. She also knew that tomorrow Tessa would be over it and Monty would likely be the first number she dialed when she got to the airport, before she boarded, after she boarded, and once again as soon as she touched down in that beautiful state of Colorado.

She loved her sister. So much it hurt sometimes. It wasn't wrong for her to want all the great things in life for Monty. But she couldn't force those things on her. Monty thought she had all of those great things. Hell, maybe she did. Maybe it was Tessa who had it all wrong.

Regardless, Tessa made a solemn vow that she wouldn't let anything stand in her way.

That included Monty. Not even Monty would stall her from grasping that new life.

❖

Marci Jones sipped a glass of red wine while her best friend, Wendy, drilled her about life. Not just any life. Marci's life.

"I know you're sick of this same conversation, but you have to agree with me somewhere deep down in that shriveled up prune-looking heart of yours." Wendy rattled the ice in her glass. "It's time to get back out there, Marci. Time to get back in the saddle."

Wendy was right about one thing. She was sick of this same conversation. Always the same damn conversation.

"Who gets to say when it's time? You?" Marci took another sip and looked around the room so Wendy wouldn't see how angry this subject was making her.

The restaurant was crowded for this early afternoon. The vacationers were beginning. Soon, this beautiful old town at the base of the mountain would be crawling with shoppers and skiers and the normal adrenaline junkies.

She loved this state, this city, and for sure, she loved the resort that Wendy and her twin brother, Landon, took over after their parents' retirement.

Marci had grown up on this mountain. This resort was her first job. Her summers and winters had been spent learning to ski, learning how to earn a dollar by cleaning rooms and vacuuming hallowed halls, and especially shoveling snow off of every inch of concrete surrounding the resort.

She'd experienced her first kiss with Shelley on this very ski slope. Her first sexual encounter only a few weeks later in one of the empty rooms in one of the wings farthest away from the lobby. The rooms that were always booked last. The rooms that overlooked the face of the mountain instead of the mountain slopes that always glistened with lights at night. Every great memory had stemmed from this mountain. From these surroundings. Some from the very resort where she now worked. Again.

How she'd ever left this place, she'd never know. She'd never wanted to leave. Never planned on leaving. Yet someone had managed to change her mind. Ashley.

"Don't get testy. You know I love you. Your best interest is always my only concern."

Marci did know that. Had always known that. From middle school where they'd met, to now, after a busted marriage, Wendy was still watching out for her. If not for Wendy, she'd still be back in Arizona, licking her wounds, unable to look any of her old friends in the eye, terrified of running into that cheating ex.

Embarrassed. That's what she'd been. Ashley had committed the ultimate cruel act of betrayal. She'd fucked another woman. A woman who was at least ten years younger than Ashley. In their home. In their bed.

Worse than all of the above, Marci had come home early to surprise her wife with a date night, bundle of peach roses in her grasp, perfect evening plans, and she caught them in the act.

The image of their naked bodies would forever burn in her mind. Her Ashley. Her wife. Betraying everything their commitment stood for. Or at least everything Marci's commitment had stood for.

Even now, almost a year later, the images awakened that angry monster. The monster that had wanted to deck the bitch who had barely grown pubic hair, then shake the hell out of Ashley. She'd wanted to. She'd felt the need, the urge, to do just that. Yet, she'd done none of those things. Instead, she'd stood frozen while Ashley covered her naked flesh, her hand over her mouth, tears welling in those beautiful hazel eyes.

Her young fuck hadn't moved. No attempt to cover herself at all. No attempt to run. No attempt at anything. Calmly, she'd waited in silence, keeping a wary eye on Marci as if she expected the action, expected Marci to charge at her.

As much as the inner demon had wanted to do just that, to rush at her, to swing until she couldn't swing anymore, the calm voice inside her head, the one that had never led her to trouble, had won that mental battle.

She'd closed the bedroom door, dropped the flowers on the carpet, and walked out the front door to the sound of Ashley's voice screaming out her name.

There was no looking back. She couldn't. Her pride wouldn't let her.

So she did the only thing left to do. She called the one person who knew the call would come sooner or later. Who had warned her. Repeatedly. She called Wendy. The silence on the other end of the line only proved that Wendy had said the words in her head instead of out loud.

I told you so.

She spent a week at a hotel, quit her job, changed her phone number, and arranged for a close friend, one who wasn't a huge fan of Ashley, to meet her at the house to pick up her personal belongings while Ashley was at work.

Another week went by while she packed her belongings and had them shipped ahead of her to the resort in Colorado, while Ashley moved out, to where, she didn't know, and didn't care. And finally, she was on a flight back home. To the home she should have never left. A home that Wendy begged her not to leave. But Marci had been in love with the hottie who'd spent her vacation at the resort. The hottie who had talked Marci into leaving her perfect world behind. Leaving all of her hopes and dreams and goals on that snow covered mountain.

What an idiot she'd been.

"Are you listening to me?" Wendy rapped her knuckles on the table.

Marci took another sip and inhaled. "Can't we talk about something other than Ashley? Why do you always have to bring her up? Aren't you sick of this broken subject?"

"Because you're avoiding it, that's why. You've become a hermit. You're mean and spitey, and fucking these tourists every weekend isn't helping you get over the fact that your wife screwed you over and broke your heart."

Shattered was more like it. Yes. Shattered. That's how she felt. Pieces. She was in pieces. That pissed her off just as much. That she'd allowed Ashley to break her. That she'd allowed anyone to break her.

She was strong. Independent. She loved people. And she used to trust openly until someone gave her a reason otherwise. But not anymore. Now, she trusted no one, immediately. She wasn't very proud of this new personality, but for now, it was the only defense mechanism she knew. The only one that felt right.

And Wendy had a point. Marci had become spiteful. She trusted no one. Fucking the women she would never see again was exactly how she wanted to live the rest of her life.

Yet there was always something nudging at her brain. Something pecking at her memory. Wasn't that how she'd met Ashley? Hadn't Ashley been one of those vacationers? One of those tourists? Hadn't she been one of those weekenders that Marci would never see again?

Sure. But things were different now. She didn't have a heart for anyone else to break. Ashley had taken care of that. She'd made sure that no one else would ever get close. And Marci hated her for that too.

"Stop, Wendy. Just stop."

Wendy leaned back in her chair and sighed. "I'm so sorry."

Marci looked up at the seriousness in her voice. "Sorry for what, exactly? There are so many reasons." She added a smile to lessen the sarcasm.

"For not fighting harder to make you stay. For not finding a way to reveal her true colors before she got her claws in you."

Marci looked away and focused on the waitress disappearing through the swinging door of the kitchen. "No one could have changed my mind."

"She was a loser and everyone saw it but you."

As much as Marci wanted to agree with her out of bitter anger, Wendy was wrong. There had been great times with Ashley. They'd planned a wedding, moved in together, went on a few great vacations, to name a few.

Fact was, when they were good, they were indestructible.

But when they were bad, they were hell-bent on Armageddon. Actually, that had been Ashley. Hell-bent to turn minor into major. A molehill into a mountain. And Marci had been determined to be the calm in her storm. Desperate to fuck her back into the calm, loving Ashley. And usually, it worked. Until it became a pattern. And even then, Marci still wrangled up the same outcome.

Eleven years' worth of those ups and downs, but until the end, Marci wouldn't have changed a single day. She'd been in love. Had built a life with Ashley. The life that was destroyed now.

"It's over, Wendy. I'm here. She's there."

"You're wrong, my friend. It's not over. You're not here. Not all of you, anyway. You left the best pieces of you back in Arizona, and I'd appreciate it if you'd go back and pick them up. And spit in her face. For me."

Marci snapped her sights back on Wendy. Yes, it was over. She'd put her house up for sale, sold everything she owned, and blocked all paths for Ashley to get to her because she damn well would never have enough balls to show up at the resort. For sure, what they had was over.

Wendy stirred the ice cubes again. "You hate her. What she did broke you. Broke your soul. Until you put yourself back together, it won't ever be over. And I fucking miss you, so sue me for being pushy and demanding and all in your business during your healing process."

Marci was touched. Wendy was her best friend. They went so far back she couldn't actually remember where the beginning had started, only that Wendy was one of the first people she spoke to after her parents moved her to Colorado. She loved her instantly. Wendy had been the constant in her life. The one who never held back when it came to her opinions. That opinion had been so loud about Ashley, it had created a deep wedge in their relationship. One that Marci had to continuously hold together, even when Ashley was trying to tear it down with her bitterness and immaturity.

Somehow, they'd managed to survive the distance with phone calls and yearly trips that Marci was forced to make alone. Ashley hated the cold. Hated Colorado. And hated Wendy even more.

"I love you." Marci reached out and squeezed her hand.

"I love you, too. But I'm worried about you."

Wendy's cell phone chirped. She briefly poked out her bottom lip then dismissed herself from the table.

Marci scanned the room. Was Wendy right? Had Ashley broken her for good? Had she damaged Marci beyond repair? And was it so bad to ride out the waves with a stranger in her bed in the meantime? She didn't think so. Nor did she care what Wendy thought. This was her personal self-medication. And right now, it was working.

"This can't be happening!" Wendy dropped back in the chair, breathless. "Selena is being admitted into the hospital. She was having contractions and they had to stop them. Bed rest until the twins arrive. What the hell am I going to do now?"

"Cancel the contest?" Marci asked with glee.

The event planner contest was all she'd heard about since Wendy and her brother had concocted the whole idea as a way to staff the newest resort. The construction was just about complete, and instead of doing the boring interviews, they decided that a little adventure along the way, and a means to bring more people to the resort to see the newest housing, would be far more fun.

They had ironed out all the details, and before Marci knew it, the wheels were in motion.

Not that any of it pertained to her. She had a cushy job, in an office, behind a closed door, where all she had to do was make reservations for people calling the resort. No sales pitch. No urging people to spend their vacation at the resort, old or new. Just answering phone calls for those already prepared to spend their time on a snowy mountain. Easy. And alone.

Sure, Wendy had stuck her there to keep her away from people. Marci was more than fine with that. She didn't want to deal with real people anyway. She didn't want to deal with people unless it was a female screaming under her tongue. And she dealt with those as often as she could.

"Don't be a smartass. I'm serious!" Wendy wrung her hands, picked up the cell phone, laid it back down, and went back to wringing her hands. "What am I going to do? I can't be a liaison for these group leaders and be their boss at the same time. I legally can't be both."

"You have tons of people working for the resort. Just ask one of them if it's that easy." Marci took a long sip of wine, hoping they could wrap up this dinner soon so she could swing by the club. With the crowd already thickening, surely she could find someone to help her forget this conversation ever took place. The one that seemed to take place far too often lately.

"It's not like I have extras just lying around. I need someone who can handle multitasking every week. Reservations. Placing orders. Running errands. For eight different groups to start off. Oh my God!" Wendy picked the cell phone up again and sent several texts before she went back to wringing her hands. "I can't believe this is happening. Monday. Every participant will be here on Monday."

Marci could see Wendy was about to blow her top. Wendy was almost always calm. Rarely ever did Marci see her lose control. "Calm down. Everything will be fine. You'll find someone."

The phone chirped and Wendy yanked it up then she sank even deeper into her seat. "Mike is out of town. He can't help."

"What about Randy? You said he left on good terms. Maybe he would come fill in."

Wendy grinned and started punching buttons on her phone. "Yes! Cross your fingers."

Time seemed to stand still while Wendy sucked at her ice cubes and stared at the phone.

Finally, it chirped, and once again, Wendy deflated.

"He's working for a wedding venue in New York now." Wendy tossed the phone on the table. "I'm screwed. I'm totally screwed."

"I'll do it." Marci spit the words out before she could change her mind.

Wendy cut her gaze around and then giggled. "Thanks, bestie, but I need a people person. Someone who can smile and talk nice and actually pretend to like the human race. Not a man-eater living off tourists."

Marci shot her a "fuck you" glare. "I said I'll do it. You better say thank you before I take it back."

Wendy narrowed those dark blue eyes. "You're being serious?"

"Yes. I'm being serious. How hard can it be to babysit a bunch of grown toddlers and make a few extra phone calls?" Marci wiggled her brow.

"These professionals are far from toddlers." Wendy leaned toward the table. "But you *could* do it. I mean, all they need to do is bring you their itinerary and you can make arrangements and reservations per their needs."

"See. I told you. Easy."

"Don't tease me, Marci. I'm freaking the hell out." Wendy gave her that serious expression, the one that teetered on uncontrollable tears or hysterical laughter.

Marci downed her drink and checked the time. “I’m not teasing. They give me a list, I make phone calls. I don’t have to hang out with them. I’m not their boss. Easy. Stop panicking. I got this.”

“And you’ll be nice?”

Marci snorted. “I didn’t say that. I just said I’d handle it.” She blew a kiss toward Wendy. “And I will handle it.”

Right now, she just wanted to get to that bar.

Sex and a passage out of her thoughts was all she needed.

Chapter Two

Marci tipped up her Yeti and took a sip of coffee before she settled in the chair at her desk to go over the files that Wendy had hesitantly dropped off less than an hour ago.

"This is your last chance to back out of your offer," Wendy said, her lip slightly curled out in a "I will die if you back out now" warning.

Marci had plucked the folders from her grasp. "I'll be a glorified secretary babysitting a gaggle of kindergarten brats. What could possibly go wrong?"

"Your mouth. That's what could go wrong."

"What? You don't believe I know how to be nice?" Marci playfully rolled her eyes.

Fact was, Wendy was right. She was rarely nice anymore. She was still scorned. Still carrying the grudge. Still angry. And she could be all of those things for as long as she damn well wanted.

"I believe you know how to. But that's different from actually doing it."

Marci tipped the Yeti back up and eyed her over the rim.

Would she ever shed this battered and bruised skin that an ugly separation had poured over her? Would she ever trust again? Would she ever look at another female without knowing they had the potential to bring her to her knees?

Deep down, she hoped one day she could loosen this barrier around herself. For now, she needed the cocoon of protection. It was all she had left.

"I promise your children will be safe from my wrath." Marci picked up a file and glanced over the tab. Tippy Franks. Thirty-eight. Atlanta, Georgia. Wedding planner. She flipped open the file to find a picture of Tippy taped to the inside cover. Dark hair. Thick glasses. Bright, wide smile. Not her type. "Besides, all I'm required to do is set up reservations, right? It's not like I'm anyone's boss. They don't answer to me. All bullshit will be handled by you. For sure you don't want me to handle drama." She looked up with an arched brow.

"Absolutely not." Wendy shook her head. "They will report to you when they have ironed out their plans. All you need to do is square away reservations. Florists, deliveries, to name a few. Nothing you can't handle from that chair."

"Perfect. Now stop panicking. I told you, I got this."

Wendy raced around the table and bear-hugged Marci from behind, chair and all. "I love you so much for doing this. You're my saving grace right now."

Marci patted her arm. "Don't get too happy. The first person who brings drama to my door will be kicked all the way down this mountain and land right on your doorstep."

"Deal!" Wendy squeezed again and trotted from the room.

Marci turned her attention to the next file.

Derrick Mathers. Photographer. Ohio. Group number three.

Next file.

Kara Blackwell. Caterer. Pennsylvania. Group number six.

Next. Next. And then next, she read through their credentials, what team they would be on, who was the leader, and who was the most experienced. She could almost see who would overtake every part of the contest by simply reading all the great things they had done with their talents.

Her thoughts went back to that long forgotten dream. Some of these people, with the same experience, could have been professionals she'd have liked to hire. People who excelled in their careers. Who had unwavering recommendations and excelled in their careers.

Some of these people could be working for her right now. Making her dreams come true.

Dreams she'd abandoned for a piece of ass.

Marci shook out of her thoughts, determined not to let Ashley in today.

She picked up another file. Tessa Dalton. Wedding planner. Peoria, Arizona.

Marci's breath staggered. Her hands trembled.

Her town. Her state. Where she'd created a new life for herself and Ashley.

Where she'd bought a house to prove to Ashley that she was serious about staying. Where they'd gotten married.

Where Ashley had ripped her in half.

Marci laid the file down, unable to open it, afraid the fragments of her life would be tucked inside. She took a long sip of coffee, hoping the flavor would calm her unraveling nerves. Ridiculous. She was being ridiculous.

Why? Why did Ashley have to do that? Why did she find it necessary to stab Marci in the back? Why?

Was it too much to ask? Was there even an answer? Did Ashley know why?

Did Marci truly want to know?

The answer wouldn't change a thing. She'd never go back. She'd never look back. But something deep down inside always came back to that question.

Why.

She slowly picked up the file again and studied the name. She should open it. Get to know the woman who would be spending the next eight weeks getting under her skin. She was being petty. She knew that.

But was it too insane not to want anything to do with Peoria? Or Arizona? Or anyone from there? She left her life behind there. Her shattered life. All that desert heat, her marriage, and the heartbreak, she'd left in her rearview mirror. Now if only she could leave all the images and memories there as well.

Once again, she focused on the file. Tessa. She didn't recognize the name. Likely she wouldn't recognize the person either. All she had to do was turn over the cover.

But the longer she stared at the manila folder, the more those angry vibes simmered in her gut.

She mentally encouraged herself to open the file. It was just paper, after all. And the person on the inside was just that. A person. A person who just happened to live in the same state, in the same town, as she once had.

She hated Arizona. It was hot and muggy. Dry and barren.

Yet, she'd never turned around. From the second she'd touched down on that hot summer day to find Ashley waiting with that big smile, she'd never turned around.

What an idiot she'd been.

Tessa's name stared back at her, daring her to turn the page, to crack open her life, to read all of her accomplishments, and to know exactly where she stood in this game.

Dammit. Not tonight.

With a grunt, Marci tossed the file away without opening it and shoved away from the desk. She didn't need to know anything about this woman. Not right now, anyway. Not when the memories were threatening.

That little bar was calling her name. She always found just what she was looking for there. And tonight, she needed to find a willing piece of ass so she could grind against it. A woman to make her forget she was damaged goods.

And now that the day was over, it was time to go find the one to make her forget.

An hour later, she scooted onto a stool at the bar and greeted Tina, the owner and quite often the bartender as she liked to get to know the patrons, even those she would likely never see again. "Hiya, lady. How was your week?"

"Tourists are starting to pick up." Tina scooped ice into a glass, poured in Jim Beam, finished with a splash of pineapple juice, cherry, and a straw, then pushed the drink in front of Marci. "You?"

"Same shit different day." Marci stirred the drink before she took a sip and moaned as the flavors burst on her tongue. "Delicious. As always. I needed this today."

That she did. Her hands were still shaking from the flood of memories spurred by a single name on a folder tab.

Arizona. Where she'd transformed her life. Where she'd started a brand new future. Leaving her old dream for a future behind.

If she'd stayed right here, if she'd not run after Ashley, she could be well into her own career by now. It had all been planned so perfectly. Event planners, caterers, photographers, all working for her, taking care of elite clients, each looking for their own personal adventure without the hassle of reservations and phone calls. Who just wanted someone to take care of everything, right down to their meals. And especially someone to keep their identity a secret.

She could have had that. An après-ski, of sorts.

If only she'd refused to back down from her own life goals. If only she hadn't tripped over her own tongue. If only she'd been stronger.

She wouldn't be sitting in this bar, all alone, scorned and torn and pissed, and wondering where she'd gone so terribly wrong.

With a huff, she took another long swallow.

"Bad week?" Tina asked while she towel-dried glasses and stored them away.

"Bad week, month, year, life," Marci said. "And to add to my own destruction, I moronically volunteered to help Wendy with the contest. I'll be babysitting a gaggle of grown misfits all fighting for a position at the resort."

"Ouch. Why would you do a stupid thing like that? You don't even like people." Tina giggled and held a glass up to the light for inspection.

Marci knew Tina was only half joking. Truth was, she was pretty transparent since she'd been back. Too obvious. All of it was true. She didn't like people anymore. Didn't like meeting strangers. Didn't like conversation. Once, she used to be the life of the party. Once, she used to smile. Once, she wasn't so guarded and untrusting. Once.

Now, she was that person. Unapproachable.

"There are a few people I like." Marci turned around on her stool and scanned the dance floor. "For just a little while, at least."

Women ground against each other as they moved to the beat while some shot pool in the far corner. A select few lovebirds snuggled and giggled at their high-top tables. If only they knew their fate, they would all walk away now and save the heartache.

Tina gave a low whistle of approval from behind her. "Check out what just walked through the front door. Oh, how I love tourist season."

Marci followed her gaze and sucked in a breath as she found the woman in question just inside the door.

A beautiful creature. All five foot four of her. Long dark hair spiraled out from under a tan slouchy beanie. A deep shade of red adorned the woman's full, pouty lips.

Marci watched in awe as the woman took off her coat to display a sheer champagne colored button up shirt. The blouse was open just enough to tease her audience with the deliciousness that lay beneath. Her green gaze raked around the room while Marci was held frozen to her stool.

She'd never experienced such first glance sexual attraction before. Not even with Ashley.

Sucked that almost everyone else around this beauty was experiencing quite the same effect. Two women approached the woman, no doubt filling that pretty mind with only God knew what kind of crap come-on lines.

The woman must have politely declined whatever pathetic offer they had concocted as she gave them all a radiant smile and then made her way toward the bar, leaving them to watch her walk away.

Marci held the woman tight in her sights as Tina gave a hungry growl behind her.

"I sure could like that one for a little while," Marci confessed.

Tessa slowly walked across the room, searching for the one who made her lick her lips in heated lust.

Tonight, she needed flesh on flesh, strangled moans, all from raw, never going to see you again sex. For the next eight weeks of her life she was going to insert every bit of her soul into winning this contest, and then a new world was going to swallow her whole.

Nothing could stand in the way or knock her off track. Not Michelle. Not even Monty, who had already called her twice since her plane landed four hours ago. She didn't have the balls to tell Monty she was going to play one of her tricks tonight. Fuck them without even bothering to ask for their names or their marital status.

Tonight, names would not be required. She wanted sweaty skin against her, fingers inside her, and a scream penetrating out of her.

Nothing more. Absolutely nothing less.

She needed to be driven sexually out of control. Just for tonight. Even if it was against her own morals.

And the hottie perched on a stool at the counter could hold the golden ticket.

The woman had a tight grip around a mixed drink, a clench to her jaw, and was holding Tessa tight in her view. Exactly where Tessa wanted to be.

"Would you like to dance?" A woman approached. Tall. Handsome. One second too late now that Tessa had her attention set on someone else.

As tempting as the offer was, Tessa already had a mission, and that mission was still watching Tessa with a curious glint in her eye.

"No, thanks," Tessa politely declined and continued walking toward the bar.

No use wasting precious time when there were so many more delicious alternatives than eye-fucking each other.

Normally, she wouldn't be hell-bent for a piece of ass. That behavior was out of character for her. That was Monty's domain.

But she was no longer in her safe place. Tonight, she wanted to take one of these butches up on their offer. Quickly and without hesitation. She was on vacation, after all. She deeply believed in one-night stands. For tonight. No rules applied here. So tonight, she was looking for something different. Someone who wasn't willing to throw themselves at her feet. She didn't want to shun those looking for love. To each their own. But truth be told, love was for suckers. For those who thought love was everlasting. Fact was, love wasn't everlasting. It only lasted until someone snuffed out the candle.

She didn't want a candle tonight. She didn't want a twinkle of love in their eyes or fake promises. She wanted a growl on their lips and nothing but pure sex on their mind.

Her gaze stumbled over the remaining women at the bar, likely the single ones, until that one face, still watching her, made her walk faster. Those eyes were making all the right promises. Promises that said no talking would be required.

Sexy brown eyes followed her as Tessa moved down the line of stools. Chiseled jawline. Firm posture. And all alone, bellied up to the bar. Exactly how Tessa needed tonight's fuck to be. All alone.

Marci reminded herself to breathe as the woman passed her by, gave a slight smile, and took a stool three spaces down. Jesus. She was gorgeous. A complete package. From that sexy stride to those fuck me eyes, she was perfect.

Time seemed to slide by as Marci watched several women approach the beauty, all leaving empty-handed, thankfully. None seemed offended. Disappointed, sure. Who wouldn't be?

Marci dared a glance in the woman's direction and found she had moved onto the empty stool beside her, and she was watching Marci with a curious expression.

"The mental conversation between you and that drink must be riveting. You haven't taken your eyes off the glass since I sat down."

Marci wanted to correct her. She most certainly had taken her eyes off the glass. She knew because she'd had to pry them off this woman and force them back onto the drink.

She was more intrigued that the woman had noticed anything other than the blatant invitations every few minutes.

"How could you notice with so many interruptions?"

The woman shrugged. "Great offers, I must admit. Amusing to hear what tipsy women will come up with to get in my pants. None were my type, I'm afraid."

Marci struggled not to look at her cleavage. Normally, she wouldn't care. The more direct she was, the better. But something about this woman made Marci want to hold that eye contact.

"What exactly is your type?"

"What? Or who?"

Marci considered her question. "Who?"

A smile lifted the corners of her lips, exposing bright teeth. "You. You are my type."

Marci resisted the urge to swallow. Pure lust danced in those serious eyes.

"Does he give you good advice?" The woman nodded toward Marci's drink. "The spirit in your alcohol."

Marci grinned and looked back down at her glass. Her third glass. "Jim Beam. And yes, sometimes he gives great advice."

The woman leaned in and Marci inhaled her floral fragrance. "Yet, sometimes he doesn't give the greatest advice?"

Marci was caught off guard. She took another sip. No doubt, she'd had too many. She should have left after the first, definitely after the second. The third, in her hand, was making her warm and fuzzy. Or was it those penetrating eyes? Maybe it was the unsettled need for sex that had brought her to this bar to begin with.

"True. Sometimes he doesn't give the greatest advice."

The woman reached out and wrapped her hand around the glass, overlapping their fingers. "Do you mind?"

Shocked by the contact, Marci pulled her hand from beneath the warm touch.

With her gaze locked on Marci, the woman put the glass to her nose and inhaled, then swirled the liquid. "Ahh. I hear him. He has a sexy, northern accent."

Amused, Marci turned on her stool to face the woman, wishing she knew her name. "Oh really? What's his advice to you?"

She almost regretted the inquiry. Truth was, she didn't want the answer. Not even the conversation. She didn't need the playful banter. She just needed the woman to lead her out of this bar, to a bed, where she could spend the next few hours pretending her life hadn't fallen apart a year ago. That it wasn't still a tattered disaster. That no matter how pretty this woman was, or how direct she was, she didn't trust a single thing that was about to slip off her tongue.

The woman took a sip and closed her eyes.

Marci suddenly couldn't wait to hear the answer. Knew it would be something sexy. Something hot. Something that would finally make her get up off this stool and take this woman out of here.

The woman opened her eyes.

"He thinks that you should come back to my room, slowly take off my clothes, kiss some very wet and heated body parts, then wrap my naked flesh all around you, and fuck me, until neither of us can breathe."

Marci's insides tightened while parts of her anatomy ignited.

The woman slid the glass back across the distance, her pretty eyes focused and determined.

"Question is, will you take Jim's advice?" She rose and leaned closer to Marci. "I'm pretty sure we're both looking for the same thing tonight. Sex. Just sex. I don't even need to know your name." She leaned back and studied Marci. "So, stud, you have about two minutes for me to walk back across this bar and likely get stopped by a few more delicious offers, one of which I will be obliged to accept if I find you still sitting on this stool. Because even though I'd rather grind against you, I'm not against settling for a handsome second place."

Marci swallowed hard. She'd never had anyone lay out a choice for her quite so smoothly. Fuck me or someone else will, although I'm choosing you, is what that choice said.

"Is that so?"

The woman gave a sultry wink. "The choice is all yours, sexy. Tick tock."

She started across the room while Marci sat dumbfounded. Her insides clenched with need. Her gut curled tight. And her common sense screamed to stay rooted to her seat, that a woman that breathtaking, who didn't hesitate to voice her needs and desires, could wield devastating power.

Marci watched her move farther away, her heart-shaped ass strutting in those too-tight jeans and, as predicted, she got stopped twice, each woman walked away empty-handed, before she reached her coat. Then another woman came to assist with the wardrobe. A butch. Taller than her by a good few inches. More than likely her type. She'd want her women stronger. To handle her. Oh, how Marci wanted to handle her.

"How in the hell are you still sitting in that seat right now after that delicious offer?" Tina scolded. "Are you a complete idiot?"

Marci couldn't tear her gaze away as the beauty pulled the folds of her coat together and smiled up at her new admirer.

Marci imagined herself on her knees, at the woman's feet, her face buried between the woman's thighs.

Her need was too great. The prize too golden. Truly, how was she still sitting in this chair?

The woman turned a steady glance on Marci. She angled her head, gave a slight shrug, then turned back to the woman waiting with a smile.

Marci held back a grumble as she watched the woman's new escort tuck her hand at the small of her back and lead them to the front door.

A knot formed in Marci's gut. Need, maybe jealousy, maybe downright want, whatever it was, it was tightening a firm grip until Marci growled.

The front door opened and then the night swallowed both women.

"Fuck!" Marci shoved off the stool and stilled herself from charging across the room.

She had no idea what she was going to say. Or what she was going to do. She didn't brawl. No woman was worth a bar fight. If so, she would have started with Ashley's new pup. A woman ten years younger. A twat. A fucking adolescent. Ashley had ripped her heart to pieces for someone who had barely learned how to drive a car. Fine, so she was exaggerating, but it all felt the same. Ten years younger. Fifteen. Twenty. Did cougars care? Is that what Ashley had become?

It was disgusting. Humiliating. Yet, here she was, all this time gone by, still letting thoughts of them together get the best of her.

She could have lost her shit. She could have gone into a rage. And she would have enjoyed it beyond measure. But what good would it have done? What good would come of her in handcuffs? No damn way she could have given either Ashley or her fuck toy the satisfaction.

Yet she wasn't satisfied with the alternative ending either. Simply walking away and never looking back.

Marci pushed away from the bar and started across the floor. She was charging toward a woman with no clue what was going to come out of her mouth, no clue how the night was going to end.

For once, she didn't care. God, it felt great not to care.

She pushed through the front door and barged into the night to find the woman leaned against a Jeep Liberty. Alone.

A smile lit her face as she cocked her head to study Marci.

Marci was going to make a very bad mistake. And she was going to enjoy every minute.

"I was beginning to think Jim had given you very bad advice." The woman fisted her fingers into Marci's shirt and pulled her forward.

Their mouths met in heated passion. Lips parted with groans and tongues invaded.

Chapter Three

Tessa was shoved against the back of the hotel room door. The rental car key hit the carpet with a soft thud as the woman's mouth crushed against her own.

A moan slipped past her lips as the woman's tongue invaded, swirling and tasting and driving Tessa's knees to buckle.

She draped her arms around the woman's neck to disguise her weakness, overcome with heat and wet need.

She suddenly wished she knew this hottie's name. So she could scream it. Why, she wasn't sure. Monday would begin a new life for her. An eight-week fight for that new life. There was no reason to know this woman's name. She wasn't part of Tessa's future equation.

Yet, the need to know remained the same even though she had no desire to share her own. This was her new adventure. Her new world. She wanted to keep it private. Keep it all to herself for just a little while longer.

No one knew her here. No one knew her name. She liked the mystery of the game.

The woman roughly bucked into her and Tessa cried out. Their tongues danced while the woman unhooked Tessa's arms from around her neck and shoved her coat down and off her arms. She impatiently began working the buttons of Tessa's shirt, and finally the material fell apart. Cool air feathered across her stomach and then warm hands fanned around her ribs, climbing higher until she thumbed Tessa's hard nipples through the thin lace of her bra.

Those hands memorized her as they curved down around her hips and then reversed their path, stalling once again to tease their pebbled creation.

Her insides tightened as the woman pulled the lace away to expose a hardened nipple.

"What's your name, sexy?" The woman ducked and captured a nipple between her lips.

"Call me anything you want." Tessa ground her hips as fire whipped a path to her crotch.

The heat was incredible. The mystery of the games even more wicked.

She'd never had sex with someone who didn't know her name. It was kind of hot.

"Sexy it is." The woman pressed herself against the whole length of Tessa. Tessa needed to feel the heat from her, needed her to be inside. Deep inside.

She fumbled with the button of the woman's jeans, her fingers snaking down inside the denim.

The woman grabbed her arm and pinned it above her head. "My name is Marci."

"Marci," Tessa whispered.

Marci groaned which only fueled Tessa's desperation to get her naked, to come against those lips. She needed to be tasted. Fucked. Wanted rushed sighs ripped from her chest.

She also wanted to scream at the woman for revealing her name, to tell her that there was an inferno scorching her from the inside out, that a sexual emergency was teetering on the horizon if she didn't hurry the fuck up, and that she'd screwed up the mystery of this entire moment by saying her name.

Instead, she ran her tongue along Marci's bottom lip and settled into the sexy way Marci was hovering over her. The way she was pinning Tessa in place with her strong grip.

With her free hand, the woman pinched Tessa's nipple, twisted, and then smiled when Tessa hissed and bucked into her.

Heat. Dear God, the heat was going to burn her alive. She wanted Marci inside her, bucking and fucking and driving her to climax. She didn't want to take things slow. She didn't want to savor this moment or make it last. She just wanted to fucking come.

"Well, Marci, now that you've broken an unspoken, never going to see you again, so names do not apply, one-night stand, rule," she pulled one of her wrists free and fisted her fingers into Marci's hair, "you are required to make me scream it."

With a firm grip, she pushed Marci down to her knees.

Marci didn't know there was an unspoken rule in the tag and release world of one-night stands. Obviously, she was out of the loop. Obviously, she'd been playing house too long.

Regardless, playing by the rules of this beauty was going to be a piece of cake. Was going to be her ultimate pleasure.

Marci snagged open the button of the woman's jeans and pulled down the zipper. She watched those lips part in heated expectation.

With her gaze locked on those green orbs, she lowered the denim and the dainty pink underwear down her legs, waiting while the woman lifted her feet so Marci could discard the material, and then nuzzled her face into the alcove of lean thighs.

The woman's chest rose and fell as Marci watched her, awaiting her invitation. A plea would be even better. But she'd settle for a simple nod. "Yes," she whispered.

Marci licked her lips, pushed the woman's legs apart, and deliberately inhaled.

She stared back up at her and asked, "May I?"

The woman nodded, her breaths now ragged.

Marci pushed a single finger into the alcove and teased the woman's clit.

The woman flattened her hands against the door, her body stiff, anxious, and prepared.

A smile threatened Marci's lips. This goddess was fighting self-control. She wanted her to beg.

Her gaze dropped back to the woman's crotch, her finger still teasing and caressing. "I'm waiting, Sexy."

"Do it," the woman begged her.

"Do what?" Marci asked.

"Put your lips on me. Make me come."

Marci slowly dragged her tongue along the length of the woman's clit before she gave a single suckle against the tip.

The woman sharply inhaled and Marci's insides clenched down hard.

She was almost desperate to give this woman relief. To hear her cry out her name. To make her cry it.

She repeated the motion all over again, teasing the woman's clit, taunting her into incoherent sounds, before she smothered her face into the woman's crotch and captured her clit.

Fire whipped through her insides as the woman fisted her fingers in Marci's hair. She pulled harder, holding Marci in place.

Marci nursed fast, then faster, before she slowed her pace, giving the woman a second to catch her breath before she started again, this time with long, barely there suctions. The kind that made the woman hitch her hips forward in angst, in search of the pressure, of Marci's lips.

"Oh, God." The woman hissed through clenched teeth.

Her knees quivered as she rose onto the tips of her toes.

"No, ma'am," Marci growled.

Marci rose and lifted the woman up and around her hips by the cheeks of her ass. Three long strides took them to the bed. She laid the woman back across the bed, pinning her to the comforter.

She kneed her legs apart, teased her slick opening, and then smoothly entered her.

"Mmmm." The woman dug her head into the bed.

Marci pumped into her, arching with every stroke, driving deep, needing to be deeper, until her mystery woman tightened, her orgasm close to the edge.

Then she slowed her pace and the woman growled in objection.

Over and over, Marci continued the torture. Taking her to the cliff, pulling her back from the abyss, only to push her right back to the border.

Those sounds. Like erotic chords of music that reached down deep. Like something stirring her soul. It was incredible, actually. She didn't want them to stop, yet she did.

"Please. I'm begging." The woman groaned.

Marci couldn't hold back any longer. She wanted this woman coming and screaming. And if she was lucky, she'd get to do it all over again before she stepped out of her life just as fast as she'd stepped into it.

Marci withdrew and dragged the woman onto her lap to straddle her. She quickly re-entered her.

The woman whimpered as Marci fucked her, as she palmed her ass, spreading her, controlling her, encouraging her to ride faster.

And she did. Faster. Rising and falling, Marci filling her, until her orgasm shattered and she screamed out.

Marci closed her eyes against the raw sound and lights burst behind lids.

She pumped around Marci's fingers and cocooned Marci's head in her arms.

Her heart jackhammered and her insides squeezed as she drove hard inside her, fucking her, already desperate for more of those sexual sounds.

Just when the spasms simmered, Marci rolled her backward on the bed, still inside her, still fucking her, and then swallowed her final cries of release.

Minutes passed while Marci's mystery goddess clenched around her fingers and finally, she went limp, her lips still locked with Marci's, those arms still cradled around her head.

Her insides spasmed in reaction to the woman's convulsive orgasm. Dear God, the sounds were going to forever haunt her.

No matter what, she had to learn this woman's name. She didn't know why. Just that she had to know it.

She fell onto her side. "You ready to tell me your name?"

The woman opened her eyes and turned a playful smile on Marci. "We are past names, aren't we? Besides, I kind of like the one you gave me."

Marci didn't like sounding desperate. Fact was, she was very close. She wanted to repeat this woman's name in her mind later, when she was masturbating to the memories, when something other than her doomed life had control of her thoughts.

For months, finding and fucking women had come easy for her. She held no further intentions for them past the sexual encounter. She could have spent the entire night not knowing their name. This one. The one beside her, who felt so alive writhing from every touch, she wanted to remember this one's name. Only this one. She wanted to think about her and smile while her name drifted past her lips.

Marci dragged the tip of her finger around the woman's nipple. "How long are you on vacation?"

"I'm not on vacation."

Marci propped her head in her hand and continued the path around the opposite nipple. "Just passing through?"

"Possibly."

"Are you deliberately being mysterious?" Marci pinched her nipple and watched as the woman's lips parted. For some reason, it thrilled her to know that she had the power to wield some control in this otherwise puzzling woman.

If only she could sway the name out of her mouth.

"I'm on a mission." The woman rolled Marci onto her back then straddled her hips. She ground down hard. "And you're nosy."

Marci grabbed her hips and slowly bucked into her.

Goddamn, this woman was sexy. And she came so well. Marci wanted to make her do it again.

If only she knew her damn name.

"What kind of mission?" Marci resisted flipping the woman onto her back again.

She wanted to be back inside her, drawing out those incoherent babbles of release. As disturbing as the fact was, she missed being inside her. Wanted to take control of every pant, whimper, and whine.

"To spread my wings." She opened her arms to the side, closed her eyes, and let her head fall back. "And fly."

Marci watched in awed fascination. Her nipples were hard, erect, pleading for Marci to taste them. She looked downright delicious with her dark hair spilling out over her shoulders.

Unable to keep her hands off such a delectable opportunity, Marci ran her hands across her stomach, along the slender shape of her ribs, and cupped her breasts.

She leaned forward, needing flesh in her mouth again. To hear the sounds she knew she could create. To experience the sounds she'd yet to create.

With a gentle suckle, she drew the woman's nipple into her mouth.

Fingers immediately wove into her hair, gentle at first, then tighter, forming a fist, and slowly she pulled Marci back until she loosened her hold.

She put her hand on Marci's chest and shoved her back on the bed, held her in place, and then ground down over her.

Harder, she circled those hips, arching, grinding harder, her lips parted, her breaths ragged, fucking herself on Marci.

Marci fisted those undulating hips tighter in her grip, positive she'd never seen anything more beautiful. Anything more carefree.

"Make me come again, Marci."

She wanted nothing else in the world more than she wanted to do just that. To make this woman come all over again.

Marci leaned forward, wrapped her arm around her waist, and flipped the woman onto her back.

Hastily, she leaned back, jerked at the button and zipper of her own jeans, needing her skin heating against this woman's skin, and worked them down and off her legs.

When she looked back down, lust and need danced in the woman's eyes.

God help her, she wanted to crawl inside her. The need was so great it made her ache.

She tugged her shirt and sports bra over her head then hovered over her.

The woman reached for her. "No more questions. Just fuck me."

Marci pushed her hand between them, teased her slick opening, and then drove inside her.

The woman instantly arched back, her hips dancing and grinding, and fisted her fingers back into Marci's hair like they belonged there, like she needed some sort of solid connection.

The same way Marci needed some kind of connection.

She'd never felt anything like it. This unwavering throb. This awakening from somewhere so deep she hadn't even known it existed.

Wendy would be thrilled to know that such an emotion still existed.

But the fact that she'd found it once again, something even stronger, scared her even more.

She didn't want to feel anything. Didn't want a throb or an ache. Nothing. She wanted nothing.

Feeling anything only led to one place. Darkness. Heartbroken darkness.

So she did exactly as the woman requested.

She fucked her.

All night.

And soon, she no longer wanted to know her name.

CHAPTER FOUR

Wendy wiggled excitedly in her office chair. For an hour, she and Marci had been going over final key components of the contest.

It had been determined earlier in the planning stages, that each team would start the marathon with fairly easy clients. That way, each crew was on a level playing field. They would prove their strengths and weaknesses and the point value accumulated at the end of the first week would determine which team would have access to the stunning lodge at the top of the mountain for the next client. The lodge that resembled a mansion. Eight bedrooms, indoor heated pool, Jacuzzi on a covered deck overlooking the valley, and a home theater. The house had everything a person could want or need while snowed in.

Marci had to admit it had been a little slice of heaven on the few nights she and Wendy had invited friends and family for the weekend. She'd imagined owning something just as remarkable one day.

That was until she'd chased a skirt down the map to a living hell on earth.

With a mental groan, she shoved the thoughts away. Not today. Not when she was minutes away from becoming the middleman for eight group leaders who would find out quickly that Marci was only there to make their phone calls. To make their needed reservations. Not be their friend. Or their counselor. Or anything, for that matter. To just make those damn phone calls. Nothing more. Absolutely nothing more.

"The remaining teams will get the other lodges in order of their scorecards," Wendy concluded.

"And the photographers? You said some crews didn't have their own? Meaning, you have assigned one to those crews." Marci hoped the question was legit and one she hadn't already asked while her thoughts continued to warp to a nameless goddess.

She couldn't stop the images from rolling through her mind. Hoped she got to experience that raw, unfiltered sex again. Of course, not with the mystery woman. She'd made her intentions clear. That she didn't want Marci to know her. Not even her name.

"Correct. We didn't get enough participants for each team to have their own. So the resort hired the missing photographers and they will double as the client's photographer as well as take group shots for social media. At the end of each week, if that team is still standing, they turn over one photo and a synopsis of the team's work for the weekly blog. Zoe from KDOX promised to report highlights every Monday." Wendy added a little wiggle in her seat. "So even for the teams that are eliminated, someone can still get a job opportunity. It might not be the golden prize, but it will be a step above whatever their profession is. Isn't that fantastic?"

The fact that Wendy was looking out for the losers didn't surprise Marci. Wendy always thought outside the box. She thought far ahead. She was always like that. Always pushing people to be all they could be. Always wanting to see people achieve, even when they failed. Like she was still doing with Marci. Pushing her to get back out there. Not to let Ashley have the final laugh.

Truth was, Ashley hadn't gotten that final laugh. Because the game wasn't over yet. Marci still held the deed to the house.

The house that she had at first gotten to call her own, and then soon got to call theirs. She was still holding out for the perfect offer. Not out of spite, but out of greed.

When she signed those closing papers, she would get back every dime she put in thanks to Ashley deciding that she didn't want her name on the title, that she was only keeping her apartment so her roommate could continue to stay there, even years after they moved in together. That should have been the first red flag for Marci. That Ashley hadn't completely committed herself. That after eleven years, she still held a lease in her name.

In the end, Marci was thankful for that little piece of help. For that reason, she would get to keep the entire sale price. She was owed at least that.

And then, she would finally close the doors on that part of her life.

Until then, she was going to sit back and let Ashley think any damn thing she wanted. One thing being that Marci wasn't selling because deep down, she wanted Ashley back. That soon, she would move back to Arizona. Or so Wendy had concluded. Numerous times.

"I'm so excited I can barely contain myself. This is going to bring so much publicity to the resort."

Marci gave her a side glance. "Yes. Because people crowding my space is exactly what I need."

"Hey, you're the one who offered. And if you so much as hint that you're going to take it back, I swear I'll send a sappy, I miss you so much and want you back text to that loser you call an ex. From *your* phone."

Marci scoffed. "You are the devil."

"No. Just desperate. And vengeful." Wendy pursed her lips and blew an air kiss.

"Don't worry. With or without your evil intentions, I'll behave with your precious misfits."

"Why the gloomy face, cupcake? Didn't find a piece of ass in that little bar of yours over the weekend?"

Oh, how she'd found a piece of ass. She couldn't stop thinking about it. Wishing she could go back in time so she could start those hours all over again.

This still thinking, days later, was out of character. For so long, she'd wanted to feel something. Anything. Something to indicate there was still life on the inside. Now, she couldn't stop feeling. Her insides tightened with just the thought of the woman, how she'd screamed her name, the sounds of her, the feel of her. She just couldn't stop. Not even with the conference room down the hall already starting to fill up with contestants, all she saw was the woman's parted lips. All she could feel was the drive of her hips.

Dammit. Why hadn't she asked more questions? Like, when she might be back in town. If she'd like to get together again. If she'd like to fuck again. And then again. And again.

"Earth to you." Wendy snapped her fingers.

Marci lifted her chin. "Don't I always find what I want?"

Wendy rolled her eyes. "If that's what floats your boat. Truthfully, I'd rather see you crushing out again. You know, pretending you're alive and not dead. Dating. Actually smiling."

Marci adored how much Wendy cared about her. How often she voiced those concerns. But it was getting rather old. It wasn't up to Wendy to decide when she should get over her failed marriage. When she should get over finding her wife of eleven years in the bed with a fucking pubescent.

"I'm not dead, Wendy." Marci attempted a smile. "Just doing things my way. For now."

Wendy reached out and squeezed her arm. "I'm sorry for being such a mom. Maybe this contest will keep me off your case. *For now*."

"One can pray." Marci winked.

"And thanks again for stepping up to help me. You have no idea how much I appreciate it."

"Don't thank me just yet. The first leader to come bitching on my doorstep could have this whole contest crashing down around your ears." Marci playfully drew a finger across her throat to imitate a knife.

"Don't kill your second chance, woman. I've worked my ass off to polish this silver platter." Wendy pushed away from the desk before Marci could inquire what that statement meant. "Ready to go meet these contestants?"

Marci stood. "Ready, boss."

"This is going to be so much fun!"

"Let's do it." Marci opened the door and allowed Wendy to exit first, while dirty images of hot sex with her mystery woman danced through her mind.

Her nameless mystery woman.

Tessa's nerves attempted to unravel as she waited with her crew in the middle section of the conference room.

She'd deliberately introduced herself to practically everyone in the room until she found her entire team, wanting her rivals to remember her face, to see that she wasn't afraid, and that she was coming straight for each of them.

And so far she was super impressed with her crew members.

Hunter, who was a wedding photographer hired by Wendy and the resort to capture candid shots but would also double as the client's employee to collect pictures for their vacation. He had dabbled in sport shots for his niece's volleyball team as well as a few NBA teams and wanted to make a career out of his talents one day. He had a sweet smile and didn't appear to be nervous at all.

Then there was Sally who had been working as a decorator and occasional planner for several years and even pulled off an event for a well known NFL player, with over four hundred people in attendance.

Tessa was impressed. That kind of event had to take skills, and she was proud to have her on the team.

However, Sally was a talker. A mile a minute, she carried on about everything, right down to finding her kitten, Sam Adams, in a sewage drain, how she'd nursed him back to health, and now he was the love of her life. Minus her ample guy friends who offered tons of benefits, she'd added with a wicked grin.

If Tessa could focus all that energy to their tasks, she'd be unstoppable.

And then there was Danny, an assistant wedding planner in a small town venue. He and his best friend had applied for the job on a dare when they were in college and when the owner had taken him on a tour of the grounds, he kind of liked the idea of helping to make someone's dream wedding come to life and was shocked that he had a knack for organizing and keeping things on task.

But she was most impressed with Seth. A caterer for a five-star restaurant in Washington. Even catered events at the White House, though he regretted he'd never gotten the chance to meet Obama. He had dabbled in decorating, his exact words, when in fact he'd spent an entire summer in Europe taking decorator classes. Also, he took a floral design class in Chicago, just because he was bored while visiting family members. And if that wasn't punishment enough, he was a part-time substitute teacher for an elementary school. He said if he could handle a classroom of tiny assholes, he could sure as hell handle a bridezilla. He indeed had a point as Tessa had seen toddlers act better than a few of her own brides.

Best of all, Seth had a vibrant smile, loving aura, and was super positive about their upcoming clients.

She knew they were going to go far in this event. Unless some of the other teams could top the talent she had on her squad, she doubted they would hold a candle to them.

And then she had herself. Who had been on top of the wedding venue game for more years than she'd like to admit. Planning weddings and events, even small birthday parties, was in her blood, handed down from their mother who had started out helping brides part-time. When her girls were too little for school but cleaning dust bunnies and toilets wasn't active enough for her. From the time she was a toddler, Tessa had been molded into this world. From a very small age, their mother had woven their lives into creating events for others, helping to pick out the perfect colors, how to find the best cake decorators, how to transform an ordinary table into a work of art. She didn't have a venue. She didn't have a business card. But she had taught her children how to find out what people wanted, and go five steps beyond their desires. Do the things they never thought possible. And never take no for an answer.

Just like when she was a child, adoring being with her mother, being a sponge when she talked out loud about her plans, Tessa planned to take everything she'd ever learned, over all of her thirty-nine years of life, and shove it into conquering this contest. She had every intention of wiping the floor with the other teams. There was no one who could outplan her. No one who could outwedding her. And damn sure, no one who could outdo her.

Her mother had already taught her how to outthink even herself. How to one-up herself. And then one-up herself again. Until a simple plan blossomed and flourished.

She'd been taught by the best. Trained to be an overachiever. She damn well would win this contest. Or die trying.

"I'm so nervous," Sally whispered from beside her.

Tessa wanted to scold her. To tell her to get a grip. This was war, after all. But she didn't want to act like a complete bitch before they were given their first clients.

Instead, she patted her leg and gave her best smile. "We got this, girl. Together, we're going to be unbeatable."

"Damn, skippy," Seth chimed in. "We're going to take them all by storm. They won't know what the hell hit 'em."

"No shit. We have the perfect crew," Hunter added. "Wedding and event planners, catering, decorating, photography…we have all bases covered. We've got this licked."

He extended his arm out, formed a fist, then motioned for everyone to join.

"Team Tessa," Seth quietly cheered amongst the loud chatter of the other groups around them.

Tessa liked their fighting spirit and enthusiasm. With that kind of encouragement, together they would help keep each other on point. And from Sally's hyper personality, that could come in use.

She hoped.

They all bumped fists as the door opened. A woman about Tessa's height with cropped brown hair that fell around her face in soft waves stepped inside the room. Her smile was genuine as she looked around at their faces, excitement visible in her bright eyes.

Everyone silenced and Tessa could feel a wave of anxiety spread around the crews. She drew in a quiet breath to settle her nerves and pressed a little deeper in her chair.

That new life was about to kick off. That new career was just around the bend. These people, these opponents, were nothing more than rocks on her path. She needed only to kick them out of her way one punt at a time.

And she would. Come hell or high water, she was going to reach that dream. She was already one step deep and nothing could block her way now.

The woman made her way to the head of the room where a table had been set up. She laid a stack of files on top and turned to face everyone.

The door opened again and another woman stepped inside.

Tessa felt the breath catch in her throat. Her insides clamped down tight as the memories flooded.

Raw images of their sweaty sex filtered through her mind as Marci followed the woman to the table wearing loose faded jeans and a pullover sweater. Hours upon hours, they'd spent grinding against each other, quenching their thirsty needs.

Tessa couldn't move as Marci leaned against the table, her gaze on no one in particular.

How was this possible? The very woman she hadn't been able to rip from her mind was right here, in the flesh, and not just a hot memory in her mind.

This was bad. This was very, very bad. Her beginning could be over before it ever began. Damn her need for sex. Dammit.

The shorter woman greeted the room. "Hello, everyone. I'm Wendy. I hate the word boss, but that's what I am. I'll be your boss through this incredible adventure."

Marci looked over the group until one face stopped her cold in her tracks.

The woman from the bar. The woman who had writhed beneath her for hours. The very woman she couldn't pluck from her brain. Her nameless beauty.

Marci expelled a sigh as heat gathered between her legs and Wendy glanced over at her.

"This is Marci Jones. She will be the stand-in liaison for all of my group leaders due to an emergency. Once you have your plan of action put together for your clients, you will report to her. She will square away all of your reservations and appointments, right down to setting up time slots for the ski slopes. If there are personal problems, don't take them to her. She can't help you with those. She is basically your secretary and nothing more. All she will do is point you to my office at the resort down the hill. So save yourself the time and bring all personal matters to my door."

Marci struggled to tear her sights off of the woman, off of that shocked expression, and finally she turned to Wendy and gave a firm nod.

Wendy gave her a puzzled look before turning her attention back to the group. "To start things off, I would love for each of you to give us your name and tell us where you're from and what talents you will share with your squads."

Marci glanced back at the woman. Finally, she would know her name. Why that was so important, she had no damn clue. Especially after she'd convinced herself that she didn't need that name. That she didn't want that name. But dammit, she did.

Right now, she shouldn't dare need that name. She should cry mercy to her best friend and excuse herself from this entire contest. Wendy wouldn't be happy to know her one-night stand was sitting in this room, among these contestants, fighting for a chance to work at this resort. There had to be some kind of conflict of interest.

Instead, she watched the contestants, one by one, give their name, where they were from, and if they had been chosen to be the team leaders, pretending to care anything about them. Some faces Marci recognized from the files. But not the woman who was firmly watching Marci. That face she would have never forgotten.

Finally, her mystery woman stood. She never took her eyes off Marci as she lifted her chin.

Marci gripped the edge of the table.

That name. She needed that name.

"I'm Tessa Dalton, from Peoria, Arizona."

Marci felt her breath catch in her throat. The name from the file. The name that had stirred those pain-filled memories to the surface. The very file her trembling fingers hadn't allowed her to open.

"I run a wedding venue, True Beginnings, with my sister. I'll be a team leader." Tessa smiled at Wendy then turned those pretty eyes on Marci, the smile smoothing into a serious expression. "I look forward to working under you."

A few people in the room giggled at her choice of words, including Wendy, who leaned into Marci and whispered, "Well, someone needs to do it."

Marci shifted. Tessa. Even her name was sexy. But not nearly as sexy as those serious eyes were, still tagged on Marci, reminding her that they'd looked up at her, down at her, directly at her, all while Marci worked another orgasm from her body.

Her insides trembled and she forced herself to look away.

This was going to be disastrous. Telling Wendy that she would have to bail was going to be completely disastrous. She could feel it all the way down to her soul.

Tessa had been too mysterious. Too closed. Something was amiss. What, why, she didn't know. But she felt it nonetheless.

An hour later, after all instructions had been given out, as well as their tablets that would link them to their client's video, the room had been emptied of contestants on their way to see the designated cabins where they would be living for the next eight weeks, Marci could finally breathe.

Wendy turned a hard stare on her. "Care to share what that sexual tension was all about? Did my best friend just have a moment of lust? Not that I could blame you. She was smoking hot and those green eyes were sinful."

Marci almost hated to admit that she'd had more than a moment fucking Tessa. "Wendy, you might need to find a replacement for me. I think I screwed up."

"I will roll your butch ass down this mountain if you say replacement one more time." Wendy dared her with a cocked eyebrow. "Explain how you think you screwed up. Quickly. Before I let my imagination run wild and think horrible things and kick you down the mountain anyway."

"Me. Her."

"There's nothing wrong with fantasizing. I'm sure I might do the same thing when I close my eyes tonight."

"No, Wendy. Me. Her! This weekend."

Wendy snorted. "Stop playing. You wish you had fucked up with that sexy piece of ass."

When Marci didn't break eye contact, Wendy angled her head. "You're shitting me."

Marci shook her head. "No. Not shitting. She was at the bar this weekend."

Wendy propped a hand on her hip. "Okay, so what does that have to do with replacing you?"

"Do I have to spell out conflict of interest?"

Wendy broke into laughter then tried to compose herself when Marci didn't share in the amusement. "Look here, glorified secretary. Who do you think would give a shit if she was fucking the secretary? The one and only person involved in this contest who can't do a damn thing to help her climb any rungs on a ladder. No one. That's who."

Marci was shocked at Wendy's response, assuming she was going to get a tongue-lashing and then be forced to make endless phone calls until she found her own replacement.

"It's not very ethical to have slept with someone from one of the teams. Don't you agree?"

"Ethical? Maybe not. But again, who cares? You hold no water in this game and I made that clear to everyone in the room. I promise by the end of this contest, you won't be the only one to have fucked someone else from the crews. Hell, you probably won't be the only person to have fucked her."

The insinuation made something tighten in Marci's gut. She looked away and took a deep breath to loosen its grip.

"But she didn't know that I was unimportant until today."

"And. What are you implying?"

"I'm just curious. If she knew who I was, thought she could earn some brownie points, that would explain why she sought me out at the bar." Marci felt the ridiculous punch of her words but couldn't shake the possibility that they were true.

"La-di-da look how you think your shit don't stink!" Wendy chuckled. "Are you being dead serious right now?"

Marci crossed her arms and looked away. Why was the notion so hard to believe? "Yes. I am."

"Tell me, how in the hell could she have known that you, just forty-eight hours ago, got yanked into this contest? She was likely in flight when you were agreeing to fill in." She threw her hands up. "No. Do not answer that. Dear Lord, Ashley did you in, didn't she? Now you're making up shit so you can recede into the darkness. I'm not sure you're ever going to recover."

"Don't go there, Wendy."

"Well, someone has to. You can't even get out of your own head long enough to enjoy a little thing called fucking."

Marci smiled. "I did not say I didn't enjoy it. Never said that."

God, how she'd enjoyed it. How she wanted to do it again. Very soon. But the fact remained that there was a possibility that Tessa had tried to use her. How, she wasn't certain. But people were evil. People thought they could be sneaky and get away with it. It could have happened. It likely happened right under her nose while she was too busy trying to pull another orgasm from that undulating body.

As much fun as it had been, it sucked for Tessa that her attempt was short-lived and a glorious waste of time. Good for Marci, however. She got a free fuck out of it. Hours of fucking, as a matter of fact.

"I'm seriously getting worried about you, Marci. This isn't healthy. Sooner or later, that guard has to come back down or you can bet your sweet ass you'll be adopting orphaned animals from these woods and giving them all first, middle, and last names."

Wendy was right. She could feel it. Even her gut told her she was being ridiculous and childish and too guarded. If only she could shake that slim possibility. If only she could shake that untrusting bone in her body.

"Fine. If you don't see it as a conflict, then I'll forget about it and move on."

"Great. And the only conflict I see here is when, where, and how you're going to do it again. I'd be a repeat offender for that one any day. Career be damned."

Marci pushed away from the table. "You're impossible."

Wendy fell in step behind her. "Coming from someone who tagged herself a sexy little thing, who could do it again without even so much as a stink eye from her boss, I'll take that as a compliment. Thanks."

Marci stepped out into the hall.

Oh, how she'd tagged herself a sexy little thing.

One who thought she was clever.

But she wasn't. Tessa wasn't clever at all.

Chapter Five

Tessa couldn't tear herself away from the window, away from the beauty beyond the glass. Snow. Mountains. Tall trees. Birds in flight. All with a clear sky with miles of visibility.

She was in awe of the magical picture surrounding her and couldn't wait to get out in it. To explore every inch of that forest. To follow the stream she could see trickling from the window. To just inhale all this beauty.

But first things first. She and her crew needed to watch their first client's video and get a plan of action in place. This was what she was here for. To cater to clients. To compete for the top points. To win. The exact reason she needed to remove her tongue from this pane of glass and get her ass in motion.

Outside her bedroom door, she could hear her crew excitedly chatting and moving about this incredible cottage, squealing in immature delight, as Tessa moved to unpack her suitcase. Who could blame them? They were going to be spending eight weeks in this magnificent space if Tessa had any say in the matter. And if luck and the capability to perform hard work was on her side, the view outside the glass could be a permanent picture she got to wake up to every day for the rest of her life.

Oh, what a dream that would be. What a dream that was.

She never wanted to leave. Even if she failed, even if she lost, she never wanted to leave. Maybe she could beg Wendy to let her clean toilets. She would if it meant she could stay forever.

When she finally left her room, most of her crew were already sitting around the dining table with their tablets and a large monitor set up in the middle where she assumed they were going to make headquarters.

Seth gave an approving whistle as Tessa sat down beside him. "Hey, sexy mama. You ready to lead this brigade?"

More than anything, Tessa was ready. But she was more ready to see Marci again. To get under her one more time. Maybe more if time allowed.

She hadn't been able to stop thinking about her since she left the conference room, admiring the red flush flickering across Marci's cheeks. What had she been thinking? Was she happy to see Tessa again? The same way Tessa had been excited to see her again?

If she had things her way, she was going to spend as much down time panting her name over and over and over.

"More than ready." Tessa nodded toward the monitor. "Hit that play button. Let's see who our first clients are and how we can make them the happiest people alive."

Hunter opened a tripod and locked his camera on the top. "I want a picture of us all looking at the monitor. I want to capture great minds working together to kick these other crews in the ass."

"Hell yes!" Sally cooed. "I can't wait to pluck out the losing teams one right after the other."

"Team Tessa!" Seth added. "Champions in the making."

Three hours later, Tessa flopped on the couch beside Seth and pulled on her boots. She was positive he was her spirit animal. Every idea she offered, he got it, even added ways to branch from them, adding his own glitter to the portrait.

It was amazing and comforting to see that someone else could see the visions in her mind and was willing to not only match it, but to stem from it.

And the rest were just as great at contributing with their own ideas that would work well.

The game plan was in action. Their clients, the first of the fight, the easiest in the line of challenges according to Wendy, would consist of a group of close friends who asked for nothing more than endless fun on the slopes, great food that didn't include fine dining, and whatever else her team thought the wild bunch would enjoy. Anything goes, they'd said, as long as it was legal.

Tessa was flooded with ideas. From skiing, to zip-lining, to beers around a bonfire. But just because these friends were easy, just because they would be simple to please, didn't mean they wouldn't get exactly what they were asking for, multiplied. This was her first chance to prove she had what it took to jump over the next hurdle. For her team to prove themselves as well. This was it. This was the warm-up to the finish line and this one, this very first one, would set the standard for all the rest to come.

And the crew's ideas had been just as great. All of which Tessa made sure to incorporate to some capacity. That was what teamwork was all about, after all. Sharing ideas. Deciding as a team to keep an idea or toss it. And in the end, almost every idea had been folded into their itinerary, and they were all satisfied that these guys would have the perfect mini vacation. From the second they arrived, all hands would be actively catering to their every whim, making sure their need for fun was met in every capacity. She had no doubt that her crew could handle everything.

She was excited and actually dreaded having to wait five days before their clients arrived. If not for having to put someone else in charge of handling reservations, she would already be on top of that as well. She wasn't used to handing over responsibility to someone else and really would much rather have complete control.

But rules were rules, and if she wanted to play this game to the best of her ability, she would have to follow all of the rules. Including relinquishing control.

Besides, that rule meant that she had to go to Marci's cabin. The very reason she was jerking her boots on this very second. She was anxious to see Marci again. To possibly be alone with her. To hopefully get beneath her.

Exactly where she wanted to be.

Tessa tried to slow her pace while Seth flipped through television stations. But she wanted to run. She wanted to get to Marci's cabin and lock the door behind her. She wanted to push Marci down to her knees, shove her onto a bed, floor, couch, she didn't care. She just wanted to get there.

"You sure you don't want me to take those notes to our sexy new boss?" Sally asked as she kicked her feet up on the dining room table. "I'd be more than happy to do that for you. *More* than happy."

"She's not our boss, ding dong." Hunter pushed her feet off the table. "And you're not even a lesbo anyway."

"I'd switch teams for a few rounds with her." Sally put her feet back on the table and crossed them at the ankles. She glanced across the room at Tessa. "And don't look at me like that. You'd do her too and you know it."

Tessa snatched her coat off the back of the couch and shoved her arms in. "Who says I haven't already?"

"Oooh! Boom-yow!" Hunter cried out and shoved Sally's feet off the table again.

Sally put one foot back up, her smiling eyes watching Tessa. "You wish. No one could fuck that sexy piece of ass and keep quiet about it. She's smokin' hot." She added the other foot and eyed Hunter before looking back to Tessa. "So do me a solid and let me go deliver that list. I promise to kiss and tell you all about it." She circled her ass in the chair and added a sexual moan. "Every glorious dirty detail."

Seth tucked a pillow under his head and settled in to watch a movie. "You wouldn't even know what to do if she sat her pussy in your lap."

"Woman that tough wouldn't mind teaching me every bitty thing she knows."

Hunter reached over and shoved her feet off the table. "Didn't your mama teach you manners? Get your damn feet off the table."

"I didn't have a mama." Sally hung her head.

"Oh, damn. Sorry. I didn't—"

"Sucker!" Sally pushed out of the chair. "And if our fierce leader won't let me go play with the sexy secretary, then I'm going to hang out with the other group at the firepit down the trail."

"What firepit?" Seth looked over the back of the couch.

"Shh. My little secret, pretty boy." Sally disappeared into the bedroom.

"She's going to be a handful. I can predict it already." Seth snuggled back down on the pillow.

"I heard that. And you're welcome," Sally yelled through the door. "Everyone should experience handfuls of me."

Hunter plopped down on the opposite side of the couch. "No dull moments for this crew. Between Danny sneaking off to talk to someone on that phone, to her, whatever she is, we're going to have a blast. I love it already."

Tessa stood, picked up their notes, and headed for the front door. "Just a word of advice. Don't call me for bail money."

Seth snorted. "Me either, girl. I would push my mother down a flight of stairs to save my money." His brow creased. "I swear, no one better ever tell her I said that."

Hunter hit him in the head with a pillow, which started a miniature pillow fight. Tessa couldn't help but smile. Already, she adored this crew. If they failed, at least they would all have fun hitting the bottom together.

She grabbed her scarf by the door and twisted the knob. "Please behave while I'm gone."

"Aye aye, Captain," Hunter gave a perfect impersonation of

a pirate. "Me shall keep the home fires burning furr ye."

Tessa stepped out and closed the door behind her, then glanced down the long drive toward Marci's cabin. She could see the light on through the window.

Would there be other crew leaders there this late? Had they, too, jumped on their game plans instead of waiting until morning?

She hoped not.

Tonight, she needed Marci on those knees again.

❖

Marci could only stare and nod compassionately at Donna, one of the team leaders, who had spent the last thirty minutes whining about her crew members not believing in her, not liking her, how this contest might not be right for her, despite Wendy telling the whole room of contestants *not* to bring personal matters to. But the thoughts drumming through her mind were anything but compassionate.

She repeated the phrase "Shut the fuck up and get the hell out of my house" over and over in her mind to keep from saying them out loud. All while robotically nodding as if she truly cared about anything this woman was saying.

The front door opened and she almost breathed a sigh of relief for the distraction.

She said a silent prayer that it wouldn't be Tessa. Saying another prayer right behind it, that it would be. She was dying to see her face again. Yet she never wanted to see her again.

Twisted. She was twisted. Wendy was right. She was a lost cause.

Tessa stepped through the door, glanced around at the other two leaders waiting by the fireplace, and then looked toward Marci.

Something mischievous flashed in her eyes as she closed the

door behind her.

Did she think Marci was an idiot? Did she think that Marci could boost her through this race?

Too bad if she did. Marci didn't have a clue what was going on around here. Didn't have a clue who the clients were or even how Wendy and Landon selected those clients. She was that closed off from the behind the scenes information. Hell, she didn't even want the inside scoop. She wanted as little to do with this whole thing as possible. And if not for Wendy being desperate for her help, she wouldn't be here now, with one woman crying on her shoulder, two more waiting for her attention, and Tessa only feet away. Entirely too close.

What sucked more was Tessa thought Marci had some kind of power in this game, and then she got her bubble busted when Wendy announced otherwise. Of that, she was almost certain. So why was Tessa staring at her with so much lust dancing in her eyes? So much fake lust. Did she think the link, all that sex, would lead her to Wendy? That maybe the more sex they had, the more she could sweet talk Wendy?

Fat fucking chance.

"Please have a seat and I'll be with you shortly." Marci nodded toward the flickering fire and turned her attention back to Donna, who was about to get on her last nerve.

God knew she didn't have any nerves left. Ashley had stomped on them and then set the bitches on fire. Not to mention, she hadn't expected that she would actually have to talk to any of these leaders. Wendy had promised as much. Had made it clear, actually, to a whole room full of people. Seemed Donna hadn't been paying attention. And as much as Marci wanted to stop her, to tell her to go right on down the hill to Wendy, she continued to listen, and nod.

She wasn't supposed to have to listen. At all. Take their notes, figure out who she needed to call, and then do just that. Only that. Simple. Easy.

Bullshit.

Wendy was going to get an earful very soon.

Instead of joining the other team leaders, Tessa began a slow walk along the foyer, inspecting the pictures on the walls, as if that wasn't invading Marci's privacy. Of course, it wasn't, considering those pictures were for anyone to enjoy, but the gall that she could do whatever she wanted rubbed Marci the wrong way.

Not to mention she could barely look away long enough to give Donna her attention. Attention she'd been promised she wouldn't have to give.

Tessa's tight jeans were tucked into a pair of snow boots topped with fur. A North Face coat was zipped halfway up, exposing cleavage in a black T-shirt.

She was downright sexy.

And Marci had heard her moans. She'd filled and fucked her as an orgasm ripped through her body. Her insides had clamped tightly around Marci.

Dammit. These dirty thoughts shouldn't be invading. Her sexual need shouldn't be overpowering.

Somehow, Tessa had known who she was. She'd thought Marci was some big shot in this endeavor. She had been so wrong. She'd climbed the wrong tree and had wasted every scream.

"One of them said I was weak. That I couldn't lead this crew," Donna whimpered. "They were all very mean."

Marci mentally grumbled. What the hell was she supposed to say? She wasn't supposed to be a damn counselor. She was a secretary. A glorified secretary, Wendy had said. Where did being a psychologist come into play?

"Why do people have to be so mean?" Donna continued.

"Maybe it was all just a misunderstanding," Marci attempted to sound like she gave a shit. Truth was, with Tessa so close she wanted every person in this room to get the hell out, with Donna leading the pack with her sniffles and tears. "I think you should sit down with everyone and see if you all can get back on the same page."

"How can I talk to them when they said I was too weak to win this contest?" Donna wiped the back of her hand across her cheek and loudly sniffled.

"So prove them wrong," Tessa said as she moved to another wall, face uplifted to inspect another picture.

"Excuse me?" Donna turned in her chair. "This isn't any of your business."

"Then stop crying loud enough for everyone to hear you." Tessa turned and tagged Donna in a hard stare. Snickers from the waiting leaders filtered from the living room, which only fueled Donna's angry expression.

"Are you making fun of me? Can't you see I'm clearly upset?"

"I'm not sure how you equated that I was making fun of you by encouraging you to prove your team wrong." Tessa turned her attention back to her inspection of Marci's little world, mostly snapshots from her younger years, long before Ashley had a chance to turn her inside out. She was actually smiling in those pictures. "Completely explains the misunderstanding."

"What exactly does that mean?" Donna snapped.

Without looking back at Donna, Tessa continued her harsh message. "I'm not implying anything, sweetheart. I'm flat-out telling you to suck it up. Wipe those tears, march your ass right back to your crew, and tell them all they can either get on board or get the hell out."

Tessa finally turned around and it was all Marci could manage not to order everyone out of the cabin so she could jack this fireball against a wall. Jesus but she was sexy as sin. It was downright hot how she didn't hesitate to blurt the thoughts in her head.

"Don't you dare let them think they got to you. Be a badass. Be in control of your power. These people chose you to be a leader for a reason. Show your team that reason." Tessa added a sheepish wink to smooth the punch of her words.

"You think so?" Donna wiped her wet cheek.

"Sure." Tessa turned her attention back to the pictures as if the conversation was over, while Marci's insides throbbed.

If only Marci could have said that, exactly like that. What she wanted to say would have never come out so nice. So raw with a taste of honey.

Right now, she wanted Donna and every other leader in this room to get the hell out. She wanted to pin Tessa against that wall and grind into her from behind. So bad it made her ache.

No. Dammit. She didn't. Tessa was a cheater. She'd used sex in her worthless attempt to climb a ladder. Of that, Marci was almost positive.

Donna pushed out of the chair, stood tall, and swiped the opposite cheek. "You're right. I am a badass. I'm going to go tell them exactly what you said. Thank you!"

Tessa couldn't even look at the woman. She was already gone, in Tessa's mind. A woman that weak didn't belong in this world. Didn't belong in this contest. Even her crew could smell her fear and her weakness and had admitted as much. And Tessa was going to eat her for breakfast. She was nothing more than an afterthought as far as she was concerned. But she was leaving now, so mission accomplished.

"No problem."

But the woman sitting across from Donna. Marci. That one, she for sure was also going to have for breakfast. In a delicious way. A few times if this crazy contest allowed enough room.

To keep her thoughts from making her restless, impatient, Tessa continued her tour of Marci's cabin, almost jealous. The place was twice the size of the cabins each crew was staying in. And according to the pictures on the wall and the personal knick-knacks sitting on the shelves, this was her home. That made Tessa even more jealous. She wanted a cabin. She wanted a fireplace. She wanted snow all around her. And she wanted those things all the time, not just in her goals, not just for the very few planned vacations when time allowed, which it never did because she was too busy making Michelle's career bloom while she sat in the shadows, the backbone to almost every event.

Finally, the last leader left and she was all alone with Marci.

Completely alone. Exactly where she wanted to be.

Marci eased out of the chair and made her way to the front of the desk, an unreadable expression on her face.

Tessa expected to be pulled against her. Wanted to be pulled against her. Then she wanted Marci to rip the clothes off her body, wanted her lips over every inch of her flesh, and then she wanted to end the torture with Marci's face between her thighs. She wanted that more than anything.

Her body heated with the need.

"Thank you for helping with Donna." Marci leaned against the desk and crossed her arms. "I think it's safe to say she won't last long. Although I'm certain I should have kept that comment to myself."

Tessa only nodded, her mind overflowing fast with images of fucking Marci on the desk. Being fucked on that desk.

"But there is another comment I can't keep to myself any longer."

Tessa lifted her chin. Her insides coiled tight as she imagined what that comment would be.

Get naked, fuck me, were among the top words she wanted, needed, to come out of Marci's mouth.

"I see you. I know your kind. So don't for one second think that little sexual stunt you pulled this weekend got you any brownie points in this game. Sorry to disappoint you, but as you heard, I have no strings to pull in your favor."

Shocked at the spin of her emotions, flipping from hot need to stunned silence, Tessa cocked her head and narrowed her eyes. Had she misunderstood? Surely she had. Because Marci seemed entirely too cool to be playing some kind of tough act. No way she was being serious.

Tessa had been called many things in life, but a cheater wasn't among them. People could assume anything about her, could almost get away with saying them out loud, but no one dared insinuate she was a cheater. Not on her taxes. Not even on a dead-end relationship.

Even her own sister was on her shit list for being exactly that. A cheater. Or rather, for being the other woman who didn't care if her nightly fuck toy had a wife to go home to.

Yes. Dammit. She had completely misunderstood.

However, rage coiled tight in her gut as she took in a calming breath, still waiting for Marci to crack a smile, to do anything to insinuate that she was joking, knowing it would do little to silence the verbal escape of the very rage that was dancing on the edge of her lips if Marci didn't laugh very soon.

Marci's hard expression proved she wasn't kidding. That she wasn't going to smile or tell Tessa that she was only kidding. She wasn't going to say anything, because by the look on her face, she was damn well serious about the shit that had just came out of her mouth.

Tessa took in a calming breath, praying she'd heard those words wrong, knowing damn well she hadn't. But for shits and giggles, she needed Marci to say it just one more time.

"I clearly didn't hear you correctly." Tessa glared her down, daring her to say it all again. "Did you just use the word cheat?"

"I'm not an idiot, Tessa Dalton, from Peoria, Arizona. I know exactly why you were in that bar. Why you wouldn't tell me your name. Why you didn't want me to know who you were."

Marci's serious expression said all Tessa needed to know.

Tessa looked down at her own feet, hoping the distraction would quell some of her anger. It didn't. When she looked back up, that same hardened stare was looking back at her.

She stepped forward and regret settled in the pit of her stomach before she even opened her mouth. She'd truly hoped to spend some quality time screaming Marci's name again. Coming beneath her tongue. Coming around her fingers. Obviously, that would never happen again.

"In a single sentence you have implied that I was a cheating slut who couldn't win this contest from any other position than from my knees. And that you were the only ladder for me to climb." Tessa let her gaze drop down Marci's body then back up to those rich brown eyes. "You, a measly nobody, bellied up to the bar to cry in your mixed drink? You, nothing more than a glorified last-second fill-in secretary, which was likely a step up from whatever cage you came from? You should have never let your ego outshine your common sense."

Marci opened her mouth to respond, but Tessa gathered her breath and drove right back in. "You called me a cheating slut with such a straight face I am convinced you truly believe your own delusional bullshit thoughts."

Tessa stepped closer knowing it could be a mistake to get too close while so many raw sexual images rushed through her mind, while raging anger whipped fire inside her body.

Marci swallowed while Tessa's perfume invaded her personal space. She hadn't expected Tessa to get so enraged. She hadn't expected to still want her so bad, even more, with the insults leaving her mouth. Nor had she expected Tessa to look so sexy with angry daggers shooting from her eyes.

God help her, she wanted to drag Tessa to the floor and then drive herself inside those slick walls.

"So let me bring you up to speed, dumbass, since you don't know a damn thing about me. I don't fuck for brownie points. I fuck for pure enjoyment. Because I want to. Because I fucking can. But I'm no cheater. Cheaters are disgusting and they are lowlife cowards. I'm not a fucking coward either. Furthermore, this is the twenty-first century. Catch up, airhead. Women don't have to do the knee crawl to be successful. We can do it all by our little selves. So jot that ginormous fucking fact down in that tiny empty brain of yours for future reference."

Tessa erased the last step between them and jabbed her finger into Marci's chest. "And so help me God, if you call me a lowlife cheater again, you'll find out just how brassy my balls can get. Today's cheap shot was the only freebie you get, stud. You won't get another chance."

With a growl, Tessa stepped back. Disgust and a whole lot of disappointment clear in her expression. From the look of those clenched teeth, Marci would never get to fuck this woman again. With her lip curled up in disgust, Tessa gave a casual inspection all the way to her tennis shoes before slowly crawling back up her legs, stalling at her abs, before finally looking Marci in the eye once again.

Sucked so bad that Tessa was sexy as hell and incredible in bed and she would never get the chance to do it again.

"What a shame we won't get to play again. I have an unwavering habit of never making the same mistake twice." Tessa flung her client notes on Marci's desk. "I hope you and the stick up your ass have a great evening."

Marci's insides cramped as Tessa curtseyed, shot her a bird, then turned on her heel for the door.

Sexually insulted. That's how Marci felt. Like Tessa had just sexually insulted her while driving Marci into her place. No. That was more like an assault. She'd just been verbally slam-dunked.

And it had been so hot. Damn, if Tessa wasn't sexy as sin with her feathers ruffled and her beautiful face a mask of rage.

She couldn't stop relief from flooding as Tessa slammed the front door shut. A nerve had been struck. Marci had struck it with her insinuation. With her accusation. A very raw nerve if Tessa's enraged reaction was any proof.

Had she been terribly wrong? Had she let her cuts and bruises push her to make rash assumptions? Was Wendy right? Had she lost who and what she used to be?

Shit. She had.

She considered going after Tessa. To say she was sorry. To retract that ridiculous insinuation. The truth had been written in those eyes. In the way she'd jumped to defend herself. Something deep down inside told Marci she was wrong. That she'd been an ass and gone way too far. Marci's inability to trust was the culprit.

Would Tessa accept her apology? Would she understand that Marci was still trying to climb out of the black hole a fucked up marriage had pushed her into? Would she understand if Marci told her the truth? That she had no desire to be attached again. That her heart couldn't take another beating.

No. Tessa likely wouldn't accept her excuses any more than Marci truly wanted to give them. Truth was, she needed to stay far away from the sexy Tessa Dalton. Far, far away.

There was nothing to retract. Or rather, nothing she should retract.

She'd said exactly what she needed to say to protect herself, even if she no longer believed that Tessa had been out to use her.

No doubt Tessa would never speak to her again. It was best this way.

Problem solved.

Chapter Six

Marci spent the next week watching Tessa from afar, watching her take this contest by storm. She and her team were proving that they were a force to be reckoned with by going far beyond what the client asked for, all starting with the very first round, a group of friends who simply asked for slope time, bonfires, and anything fun. Tessa and her team had reached outside the box by adding a Coldplay concert with private backstage passes, a bonfire that included a full fireworks display, and scored them slope time with a group of Olympians. Marci had never seen anyone more shocked than the group of best friends, who hugged Tessa and her crew over and over and over, practically in tears to meet their idols.

How they'd pulled it all off, Marci had no clue. How they had come up with those extra plans, was epic.

They truly made the other teams look like rookies who went strictly by the book by giving their own clients exactly what they asked for and nothing more. At all.

Tessa was here to win. At all costs. It showed in the way she went above and beyond to make her clients happy. And she definitely wouldn't take no for an answer.

Marci was forced to text her for their second client to give her the bad news, that the restaurants her clients had requested couldn't accommodate their reservations, that they would be unable to make room in the dining area on such short notice, Tessa wouldn't accept that answer.

Somehow, she'd changed the owner's mind and gotten her clients in. Or rather, gone over Marci's head and gotten done what Marci couldn't. That "we'll see about that" factor was so hot. Marci liked that take-charge attitude. Too much, actually.

Tessa required very little help getting what she wanted.

What help she did need, she'd sent Seth to notify Marci. It was just a simple change in the time slot she'd reserved for the clients to take a ski lesson, but it was a great big fuck you to Marci.

Marci couldn't blame her. She wouldn't speak to the asshole who accused her of trying to cheat either.

Worse, the one time she'd gotten Tessa alone, when she had every intention of saying she was sorry, even though she'd convinced herself time and time again that she would do no such thing, she'd fucked that up too.

Tessa seemed to love the outdoors. Possibly more than Marci, which she thought was nearly impossible. No one had spent as much time as she had exploring these woods. Yet Tessa was giving her a run for her money with her numerous adventures in these white surroundings.

Marci could almost pinpoint what time Tessa would be outside walking in the woods and the path she would take. The same route she'd been taking day after day.

So Marci made sure she was along the path one day. She had to tell Tessa that she was sorry. She had to. No matter how many times her inner voice warned her against such bad judgment.

But when Tessa emerged on the trail alongside the creek, looking absolutely stunning with her hair trailing from beneath her beanie and those striking green eyes staring at her in disgust, she'd lost the rehearsed words stored in her mind. Lost every single one of them.

"Can we talk?" Marci had asked.

"About what?" Tessa's hard stare had been daring, making Marci forget exactly what and how she'd wanted to deliver that apology. The one she didn't want to give in the first place. The one her body seemed determined to give even with her conscience screaming that she shouldn't.

Whatever hidden force was pushing her, against her own heart, her own judgment, was winning this battle, and Marci felt helpless and out of control.

"I think I owe you an apology."

"Well, I'm sorry that you *think* that you owe me an apology." Tessa turned and walked away, leaving Marci to repeat the words in her head until she finally figured out exactly where she'd gone wrong. Again.

There was no *thinking* that she owed Tessa an apology. She owed her that apology. Period. And that single word had been her downfall.

Marci had watched her walk away, struggling not to chase her, regretting her words, the order in which she'd put them, that she'd used that one word in particular at all. Seemed she couldn't get them right to save her life around Tessa.

And now here she was, already planning the second attempt. If luck was on her side, she'd get it right this time.

She was going to follow Tessa to the pond house, where Tessa had made a habit of disappearing to.

Marci had found her own solace in the little two-room cottage as well. With nothing more than a kitchenette, bathroom, fireplace, and wraparound couch, it made the perfect quiet spot away from prying eyes, to be with her own thoughts, where she could actually concentrate on them.

There, she'd cried. She'd let out rage. She'd searched for the answer. Why? Why had Ashley leveled their relationship to the ground? She'd never gotten that answer, nor was she still searching for it. It was obvious that she was never going to get it anyway.

She had succumbed to searching for women to quiet her demons instead. They helped her forget that an answer was still dangling by a string, hanging in the distance, unreachable.

But right now, there was only one woman on her mind. One she wanted to taste once again. Even if she had to demolish her own standards to have her just one more time.

❖

"I can't believe you're not going to party with us tonight." Seth fell on his back across Tessa's bed and gave a pout. "Don't you want to go celebrate this fabulous victory?"

Celebrate? Of course she wanted to celebrate. But in a place where drinks would make rounds, where the strobe lights would be arcing around the room, and Marci and possibly Wendy would be feet away? Not a fat fucking chance.

She'd rather spend the evening in the little cottage by the pond, all alone, catching up on an erotic novel that could end with a little personal time with her vibrator.

Or getting a root canal without numbing medication. She'd rather do that than be near Marci Jones and her crazy behavior ever again. Crazy. The woman was crazy. And who did she think she was? A celebrity? The owner of this resort? Who? Who the fuck did she think she was that Tessa needed her to reach the top?

The past week hadn't been easy. Especially with Marci always close by, sometimes stopping by each cabin to check on the crews. Not to mention running into her on the trail by the creek earlier in the week.

She'd been so sexy wrapped in her dark coat and beanie cap, those apologetic eyes so sexy.

An apology that had been hampered by her indecision to get her words right.

She *thinks* she owed Tessa an apology? There shouldn't be any thinking involved with that decision. Yes, by God, she owed her an apology for being such a dick. For being so callous and untrusting. For calling Tessa an easy slut. A coward. And a cheater.

The nerve!

Even though she looked downright handsome stumbling over her words.

Bet she got them right the next time. Or stayed away from Tessa altogether. That was definitely the best option. She felt weak around Marci, and weak had never been part of her character. Sucked that Marci was bringing out that bad trait. Even if she didn't know it. And never would.

Besides, Tessa didn't trust herself around Marci. There was something about her that grabbed at her soul. Something that made her think of her every night when she was alone and the cabin was quiet. There, in the privacy of her mind, with the sheets caressing her skin, she could have the woman who had taken her away from the bar, the woman who had played her body like it had been made for her hands only. That woman. That was the one she drew into her mind while her hand splayed her lips open to flick her clit beneath the covers.

"I'd rather stay here and get a head start on our next clients. We get an extra day to make plans thanks to this win." Tessa patted his outstretched leg, shoving thoughts of Marci away once again. She didn't deserve to be in Tessa's head. Ever again. "Besides, I might not want to see any of you in drunk mode."

"You do have a point." Seth snorted and rolled off the bed. "Have fun with your alone time." He added a mischievous wink.

Thirty minutes later, Tessa watched the Jeep head down the hill, happy she would have that alone time. Finally, the cabin was quiet. She had the whole place to herself until tomorrow when they would return and she would be back to work as normal by afternoon, planning out an itinerary for the new clients. Unless she started tonight, which she should, but deep down, didn't want to.

She should curl up with her computer to meet the clients. To get to know them and what they expected from their long weekend. It could be a wedding this time. Could be just a family coming for vacation. Could even be a bachelor or bachelorette party.

Whoever the clients were, they would be housed in the lodge at the top of the mountain. That added bonus came from having top points of this round.

And no matter who they were, they would have to wait for tonight.

Right now, all she wanted to do was get to the cottage and spend some quiet time beside a flickering fire, cuddled up with a book.

That's truly all she wanted. She deserved just one night to herself, even if those top points, the win, would allow her one extra day to jump ahead of the other crews. Truthfully, she trusted herself and the crew members to get the job done with even half the time. She trusted their abilities that much. And that meant a single night could be spent thinking about something other than work.

She made a large mug of coffee, donned her coat and beanie, shoved the book in her pocket, then headed out into the snow, eager to get her cozy on. All alone. With her crew, though she loved them dearly, out of her hair.

The scent of pine and clean air surrounded her as she slowly made her way over the creek bridge. She stalled to watch the moonlit trickle of water veer between rocks and tree roots.

Heaven. She felt so close to heaven while standing in the middle of such magnificent nature. What was it like to live here year round? Did the forest trim down in the summer or stay just as full all year round? Was there snow three-fourths of the year? How hot was the summer? Soon, she might get all of those answers.

The thought made her giddy and she forced herself to keep moving. She made it to the little cottage that she'd found by accident while hiking one day. One of her many hikes. She truly couldn't get enough of the nature surrounding her. She wasn't sure why her crew wasn't interested in exploring. None of them had ventured outside the cabin unless they were visiting people from the other crews at this so-called firepit.

She was glad they had found other friends and was prouder that she didn't have to worry about loose lips. Sharing information in this contest wouldn't do anyone any good. Each team had different clients, and no two clients wanted the same thing.

The whole thing was set up perfectly, and she hoped she got a chance to voice her admiration to Wendy for such calculated choices before this contest was all over. Before she and her crew were crowned the winners.

Several minutes after getting the fire started and curling up on the couch, Tessa heard footsteps on the porch. She considered grabbing a fire poker, maybe even the heavy glass candleholder on the table beside her, but her gut told her there was nothing to be afraid of. That she knew who was standing beyond the door.

Hadn't she been expecting her with every trip to the cottage? Hadn't she almost willed her to follow Tessa every single time?

And now that her wish was standing on the threshold, her gut curled. That churn told her to be very afraid of who would likely walk through that door. That person made her weaker than any contest. That person had the ability to make her wet.

Without knocking, Marci stepped through the door, and Tessa had to fight not to react. Not to push off the couch and go to her. No one should look that sexy in a thick coat and beanie, but damn if Marci didn't take the prize.

Marci gave a single nod as she closed the door behind her.

"I'm impressed your ego fit through the doorframe." Tessa flipped the page of the book she wasn't reading and pretended that Marci being near her wasn't affecting her breathing.

"Can we talk?"

Tessa lowered the book to her lap. "Does it have to do with my new clients?"

"No."

"Does it have something to do with one of my crew members?"

"No."

"Am I being ejected from the contest?"

"Of course not."

"Then we have nothing to talk about." Tessa opened the book again. "So please take your fat head and squeeze it back through the door."

Marci took a timid step forward. "Look, I didn't come here for a cat fight. I—"

Tessa snapped the book shut, pleased that Marci hadn't turned on heel and left. Marci leaving was the last thing she wanted. She wanted to scream at her. Wanted Marci to tell her over and over that she was sorry. Then she wanted her to prove it. Fuck. She was so twisted it made her question her own sanity.

"No? Then why the hell are you here? Did you come to accuse me of knee walking for my clients, too? Hand job for the men, finger fuck for the women, and ding ding, we have a winner?"

When Marci didn't respond, Tessa eased off the couch, anger and need woven tight in her stomach. "You know, my grandpa always said it's the punch you never see coming that hurts the worst. He was right. But I see you now, asshole, and I warned you that your sucker punch was a one-shot deal. So please remove your paranoid ass from my view before I'm tempted to do something stupid."

Like fling herself into those arms. Like unzip that jacket and crawl inside it. Like sink to her knees and claim Marci. Yes. She'd be stupid enough to do just that.

"Would you please accept my apology?"

"What apology? The one you *think* you offered? The one you *thought* you owed me?"

"Tessa, what I said was uncalled for. It's been a really bad year, and I guess you can say I have a few trust issues. For that, I'm sorry."

"That's your excuse? That's your sales pitch? That you had a bad year?"

Marci inhaled but didn't offer a response.

Tessa eased forward, knowing she was an idiot to do so. If she got too close, the hands of sexual need would shove her the rest of the way. "Do I look like a fucking therapist? Did you come here looking for a free pass because some cheating loser broke your heart?"

Marci cocked her head. "Who said someone broke my heart?"

"You did, just now, when you used that cheesy pathetic phrase, I had a bad year. You didn't say a family member passed away. You didn't say your dog died of old age. You didn't say that you lost your job and had to seek government aid. Saying you had a bad year is a classic cop-out which means you're either a coward, or ashamed, or haven't found closure. Either way, I don't possess the proper degree for the help you require."

Marci's jaw tightened. Tessa had struck a nerve and it was rather sexy. And deserved.

"I'm not ashamed or a coward. I didn't do anything wrong." Marci lifted her chin defiantly.

Tessa liked that last part. That she hadn't done anything wrong. She hated cheaters. And she disliked people who slept with cheaters. Even if she loved her sister, she didn't have to like her or her tacky ways.

"So, like I said, someone broke your heart. And she got ugly in the process. Correct?"

Marci looked down and Tessa was tempted to reach for her. Reaching for Marci would only end with her name being ripped off the tip of her tongue. Damn, she was hot as sin.

"Yes."

"Ahh. There now." Tessa lowered her voice into a caring tone. "Do you feel better now?"

"No."

"Good," Tessa barked. "Me neither. Now, if you don't mind, I have some hot sex to get back to so please let yourself out."

Tessa turned with all intentions of curling back into those thick cushions, when Marci grabbed her arm and pulled her to a stop.

She told herself not to turn around, not to look into those chocolate eyes, at the same time she was turning to do just that, unable to resist the temptation, that tight hold making her wet instantly.

"I'm very sorry for what I said. It was immature and undeserving. Will you please accept my apology?"

Tessa considered her words, considered a few tactful ways she could make Marci earn that forgiveness.

Only one idea sat well with her.

She pulled her arm free of Marci's grasp and sat on the edge of the couch. "Since you think I need to earn my success from my knees, you can earn my forgiveness from yours."

A smirk danced along Marci's lips before she ripped the zipper down and tugged the coat off her body.

Tessa's insides clenched as Marci sank to her knees and pushed Tessa's legs apart. She stared up at Tessa as she moved in closer. With a slow grind of her hips, she drove against Tessa. She continued that carnal stare for several agonizing seconds before she leaned in and captured Tessa's lips.

Flames licked her crotch as Marci's tongue invaded her mouth, as her hips surged forward with blatant intention.

Tessa fisted her fingers in that unkempt hair, desperate to get control, desperate to lose it altogether. She wanted, needed, Marci to know she wasn't easy, that she would have to work to earn her forgiveness. Forgiveness that would have already been given had Marci simply said she was sorry. A real sorry. If she'd admitted that every word she's said had sounded like a crazy person.

Oh, but the sex they could have been sharing this entire time if she'd just admitted she'd had a temporary moment of insanity.

With a groan, Tessa pushed Marci back, immediately missing the pressure of those lips, instantly regretting that she was faced with those beautiful dark eyes packed full of passion.

How loud they spoke.

Tessa bit her bottom lip to stifle the need to jerk Marci back to her mouth. "You have one job." She fanned her legs wider. "One job."

A smile lifted the corner of Marci's lips and her gaze drifted down to Tessa's crotch. "One job."

Marci's insides clamped into a vice grip with Tessa's demand. It was downright hot how she wasn't allowing Marci to get away with her verbal abuse, with her unnecessary accusations toward a woman she barely knew.

Even more, she liked a woman who was direct and to the point. No guesswork. Just crystal clear intent.

She tugged Tessa's sweatpants down to her knees, ducked under the bridge of cotton material, and hungrily captured her clit.

Tessa bucked against her face and arched, a long hiss escaping those lips.

She nursed, alternating between fast and slow, teasing then going all in, driving and withdrawing Tessa from that sexual abyss.

"Finish me!" Tessa fisted her fingers against the couch. "I'm in pain!"

Marci teased her wet opening and then pushed inside her.

Tessa's insides gripped tightly around her and then she screamed out. Her body convulsed and her hips circled.

Marci continued to nurse and fuck her until Tessa sagged against the cushions, heaving in air, her chest rising and falling to some unheard music.

Finally, Tessa opened her eyes and looked down at Marci. Her focus remained steady as she watched Marci.

What was she thinking? Why did Marci even want to know? For some reason, she wanted to know.

Marci ducked out from under the alcove and crawled onto the couch beside her. “Am I forgiven?”

Tessa drunkenly pulled her sweats back up and pushed off the couch. She picked up her coat, pushed her hair over her shoulder, and started for the front door.

“All forgiven. Have a great night.” She opened the front door, walked through, and shut it behind her, while Marci stared in disbelief.

Minutes went by while her insides throbbed with need, while she waited, expected, Tessa to come back, to fix the wet mess between her thighs.

Fact was, she knew Tessa wasn’t coming back. She was proving to Marci that she would not be treated with such disrespect. That she would always stand up for herself. That she would always meet a bully halfway. Marci regretted that she’d been that person. That she had hurled insults when they weren’t required.

Tessa was standing up for herself right now. It was so damn sexy.

“Are you kidding me?” Marci snickered and glanced around the empty room, her crotch in heated pain.

CHAPTER SEVEN

Tessa dragged the last bag of trash to the edge of the driveway and looked back to the wicked gorgeous lodge. She was positive she'd never seen a more stunning creation. On or off the cover of a magazine. From the large open rooms to the remarkable surroundings, she'd fallen head over heels in love with this house. She never really loved things. Especially material things. Didn't love her car or give it a pet name. She was just content with good gas mileage that would get her from point A to point B without malfunctions. Nor did she really love her own house or plan to make cute remodel plans. She was content just the way it was.

But this lodge. That new adoration for a materialistic thing was on a whole new level. She loved it. Adored it. Wanted to decorate with her own style and give it a pet name. She wanted to claim it as her own, that's what she wanted. Of course, that was ridiculous and out of the question. It was owned by the resort and only the highest paying customers got to step foot across the threshold.

Maybe one day she'd make enough money to own something just as spectacular. Hopefully, it would have this stunning view as the added bonus.

And their latest clients had spent the last three and a half days under this roof.

She'd never met a more rowdy bunch. From the bachelor, to his groomsmen, to their friends, they had all tested every nerve she had in her body with their all-night parties and insane daily adrenaline junkie adventures.

She was worn to the bone and had never been happier to see someone leave.

But as happy as she was to see their time end, each of her crew members had gotten rave reviews, which gave them the highest points once again, which brought yet another win for her team. Which also meant next weekend, they'd be back in this very lodge. This breathtaking place with its panoramic views of the mountains. And exact replica of a house she longed to own one day.

Her crew was still inside the lodge cheering excitedly after Wendy's phone call to give them the news. And they were cleaning. Cleaning. Cleaning. Lord, she'd never seen such a mess in her life. Thankfully, the cleaning hadn't included patching holes or removing vomit out of carpet. How thankful she was for that.

Now all they had to do was put this amazing place back together the way it was before the rowdy bunch arrived and head back down the mountain to their cabin where Tessa would likely face-plant on her bed while the rest rushed around the house to get ready for their celebratory night out on the town.

Once again, she had no desire to attend. Not because Marci might be there. But because she likely wouldn't be. She'd likely stay on site. Tessa prayed she would. Then prayed she wouldn't.

Marci was too tempting. The incredible sex too enticing.

Fact was, she had an agenda. A life agenda. A future agenda. To win. To take this contest by the horns and be the last man standing. Her plans didn't include Marci. Her future didn't include Marci. The win meant too much to add any type of romantic interest to the mix. Not even simple sex. Especially not that. Especially with Marci. Sex with her didn't help her thought process. At all.

Two hours later, just as predicted, her crew was rushing around inside, chatting excitedly about their night out, their win, how they couldn't wait to rub it in the other teams' faces, that they had won top points yet again. That their leader was a badass.

Those words made Tessa smile as she leaned against the porch railing, trying not to look at Marci's cabin in the distance. A single light shone in the window. Was she home? Was she already at the base of the mountain? Already bellied up to the bar in hopes of scoring a midnight fuck?

The thought made Tessa uneasy. She wanted to be that midnight fuck. Tonight, that's all she wanted.

No, the fuck she didn't. Or rather, shouldn't.

Contest. Win. Win. Win. That's all she wanted. All she had time for. Marci couldn't, wouldn't, be on her road to success.

The front door opened and Seth stepped out. "Hey, chica. I shouldn't waste my time asking if you're going to join us tonight, so blame the gentleman in me when I ask if you'll be joining us tonight."

Tessa shook her head and looked away from that damn light in Marci's window. "No, sir. I'm going to catch up on some z's."

"Ah. Is that the code you use?" He winked.

Tessa almost blushed with his insinuation. "Code for what?"

He arched a knowing brow at her. "Code for sex, of course. With the tough secretary who can't keep her eyes off of you when she comes to visit, using that cute excuse of making sure everyone was okay and that no one needed anything." He bumped her hip with his. "You forget we talk with the other crews. She hasn't visited them once."

Tessa opened her mouth to reply, to lie, but he threw up his hand. "Don't you dare even attempt a denial. I'm not blind." He nodded toward the cabin where her crew was laughing hysterically over something. "They might be. But not me."

He stepped closer. "Besides, we mischief makers have to stick together."

Tessa desperately wanted to keep up the charade, but truth was, even if the whole crew knew she'd slept with Marci, she hadn't done anything wrong. Marci held no power in this game. So what if someone knew?

"Meaning?"

"Meaning, I've been sleeping with someone from one of the other crews." He moved back with a wicked grin.

"No way. How? When?"

"You want details? Well, aren't you kinky!"

"Gross. Hell no," Tessa scoffed. "Seriously. We've been working our asses off. How have you even found time?"

"Where there's a will, there's a way. Right? Boss?" He snickered. "But if you must know, his cabin is less than half a mile down the walking trail. And his room isn't connected to the main cabin." He wiggled his brow.

Tessa clearly wasn't paying attention to her crew. Or their extracurricular activities. But obviously, his late night escapes to this "firepit" weren't impacting his work ethic. He was spot-on and put everything he had into their clients.

She swung her gaze back toward Marci's cabin. That freaking glow through the woods was beckoning her. Calling out to her. Begging her, in fact.

The front door opened and the crew filed out onto the porch, each chattering with excitement.

"Come with us, Tess!" Sally said, and she scampered down the steps.

"Yes! Come party with us, oh awesome leader," Hunter chanted.

"I'm old, you guys. I need sleep." Tessa tried to sound genuine.

"You don't know what you're missing," Danny added as he followed the others down the stone path leading to the driveway.

Seth winked and stepped off the porch. "Have fun with those z's. See you in the morning. Or later." He raced to join the rest climbing into the Jeep, and soon all was quiet around her.

Except for the moon brightening the white snow across the ground, and except for the fucking light in that window through the trees. That damn light was so loud.

She was all alone. They were all alone. All she needed to do was walk the distance between their cabins, rap on the door, and her night could be spent with orgasms racking her body. Oh, how she wanted that orgasm.

With a mental grunt, Tessa snagged her coat off the porch swing. She needed to go take a walk to wipe this sexual need out of her brain. She needed the cold to seep in and put out these heated thoughts. That's all she needed. Then she would be able to give her undivided attention to their next clients. Exactly where her undivided attention needed to be. Dammit. Not on Marci. Not on the splendid sex they could be having.

Marci watched Tessa make her way toward the creek, her long hair spilling out from beneath a tossle cap, exactly where she expected her to go after her crew left.

She'd been watching her all week. How often she explored the outdoors. Resisting the incredible urge to join her, to shove her against a tree and then sink to her knees once again. She'd envisioned doing exactly that. Let her knees freeze. She didn't care.

Tessa stopped to look up at the moon. Even through the pine branches, Marci could see her chest rise with a deep inhale.

She was born and raised nearby; these mountains had always been her home. She loved the cold. Loved the cleanliness in the air after a snowstorm. And loved watching Tessa love it too.

Ashley had hated it. Hated everything about the cold. How she had wound up on vacation at a resort in Colorado with her friends was still a mystery.

Even after Marci had chased her back to Arizona, made a life with her, bringing Ashley back home was out of the question. So Marci had come alone. Always alone.

Sure, her parents, even Wendy, had come to visit her, but it wasn't the same. She wanted to share all the glorious things she loved about Colorado with Ashley. She'd wanted Ashley to see those things and love them as much as she did.

It had never happened.

But she'd loved Ashley enough to plan alternate road trips. Loved her enough to go home without her even when Ashley pouted and sometimes begged her not to go.

Watching Tessa close her eyes and tilt her head back, with the moon shining down on her beautiful face, made her miss what she'd never had in Ashley.

Ashley would have never stood in the snow in awed amazement. No matter how many years they could have been together, Ashley would have never explored these stunning mountains with her.

For the first time since she walked away from her marriage, Marci didn't feel that grip of anger at the thought of what she'd lost. Or how she'd lost it. It was comforting, actually. To not have a gut reaction at the thought of her. It was enlightening. Refreshing.

Tessa finally started walking again and Marci stepped out into the moonlight hoping her movement didn't startle her.

"What the hell, creeper!" Tessa gave her a stern stare but didn't back away.

"You shouldn't be out here alone," Marci said. "Bears and mountain lions are native to this area."

"Says the person who is out here alone?"

"I was born and raised here. I'm used to watching out for danger," Marci said with more confidence than she meant.

Tessa lifted her chin. "Well, I appreciated the warning, but they can't be any worse than the humans who act like animals."

"Ah. We're still playing hard to get?" Marci stepped toward her. "Was my apology not good enough?"

Tessa wanted to take a step back. Mainly because it would be too easy to drive herself against Marci.

She looked so delicious with her thick coat and gray beanie.

And Tessa knew what those lips felt like fastened around her, pulling her to climax.

Oh, God, how well she knew.

"All is forgiven. I just don't have any desire to be your friend." Tessa prayed the words had held more confidence than they felt rolling off her lying lips.

Truth was, she did want to be Marci's friend. Friends with benefits. Many, many benefits.

Honestly, even that was a lie. She would bet anything that Marci was a great friend. Wendy appeared to be a very bright person who was smart and seemed to possess common sense. Likely, she wouldn't have a deadbeat for a best friend.

But dammit, that kind of friend would only block Tessa's finish line. She couldn't have anything standing in her way. Not even meaningless sex.

"Good. I don't want to be your friend either." Marci motioned for Tessa to follow. "Come with me. I want to show you something cool."

She started walking, knowing deep down there was no other choice but to follow. Her natural curiosity would always outweigh her need to remain angry. Or to drag out the need to continue to make her point. A point Marci should had gotten loud and clear by now.

When Tessa caught up with her, Marci smiled and led the way to the small eight-foot-high waterfall. She stepped onto the platform of flat rocks that led behind the waterfall, looked back to Tessa, and extended her hand. Images of raw sex filtered through her mind as those eyes focused on her. The moon gave perfect light to her tranquil stare. She should tell Marci that she was sexy. That beneath nature's lamp, she was absolutely perfect.

"Don't be afraid. It's safe."

"I'm not afraid." Tessa reached for Marci's hand and stepped up beside her.

Her gaze dropped down to Marci's lips and then she looked away, fighting the emotional tug and sexual tension between them. From that look of passion on Marci's expression, Tessa wasn't in this sexual mental state of mind all alone.

Together, they walked along the wall of water, and then Marci ducked behind the flow and pulled Tessa with her.

Tessa sighed in awed amazement as they stepped behind the waterfall, with Marci guiding her down like a true gentleman, both hands on her hips, strong and steady as she lowered Tessa to her feet. The moonlight gave ample light, almost like a magnifier through the water, to the lobby of the cave entrance. Tessa took in her surroundings with baffled silence.

How did Marci know that she would love this place? That she would be in awe of such a hidden, natural made treasure? And why was the thoughtfulness reaching down deep inside her? Why was it making her feel like the treasure?

No one had ever been this thoughtful. Not a single lover, beneficial friend, or even those rare ones she'd actually called a significant other. No one.

And the warmth spreading over her right now with Marci watching her, made her want to fly into her arms, hug her, and thank her for such a priceless gift.

She stared around her in complete shock. The walls of the cave sparkled like diamonds, probably fool's gold, but their beauty held no candle to anything Tessa had ever seen before. Everything around her was absolutely breathtaking. Especially Marci.

"It's amazing." Tessa finally found a word that compared to what she felt. She was suddenly jealous of Marci and her ability to explore this entire region. With a few more weeks of hard work, she hoped to do the very same thing. Explore. To thank the creator for such magical wonders. "How did you find this place?"

"Too much time on my hands?"

Tessa dared a glance in her direction. She heard loneliness etched behind her words. What had her ex done to her? Whatever it was, Marci wasn't over it. But this was a damn good way to help forget whatever horrible thing she'd experienced at the hands of her ex.

Tessa smoothed her hand along the wall. "It's truly incredible."

Marci walked up behind her. Slow and deliberate.

Tessa stiffened. Marci's aroma surrounded her and she had to close her eyes against the fire whipping along her limbs. Her body hummed with life as Marci's breath feathered against her neck.

"Look," Marci whispered.

Tessa's insides clamped with the sound of that whisper. How did Marci have the power to do that? To weaken her knees with barely a sound?

Sudden brightness in front of her made Tessa open her eyes. She found Marci's phone flashlight highlighting the wall, displaying etches in the rock. Native American markings, or something very similar. Aged but visible.

Overcome with heartfelt emotion, Tessa reached out to trace the carvings with her fingertip.

Hundreds, thousands of years ago, someone had stood in this exact spot and painted a picture with possibly nothing more than a rock, for Tessa to witness one day.

And what exactly was the message they wanted to give?

Marci kissed Tessa's neck. "You like them?"

Tessa angled her head, welcoming the hot suction. She didn't want to move. Didn't want to make Marci work for another apology. All she wanted now was Marci's naked flesh against her own.

She turned in Marci's arms. Instantly, she was shoved against the rock wall. Marci's mouth clamped down around her own. She groaned and ground her hips into Marci, almost desperate for contact.

True, she shouldn't be here. True, she should be back at the cabin getting to know her next clients. True, she should be getting her ducks in a row for the next kill.

Also true, she didn't give a shit about any of the above right now.

The only thing she needed at this exact moment in time was Marci to jerk her pants down to her ankles and then drive inside her. Tongue, fingers, body, she didn't care.

She needed Marci controlling her every breath. Every gasp and pant of pleasure. She needed that so bad it made her soul quiver.

As if she'd read Tessa's mind, Marci ripped at the zipper of her coat and tossed it to the side.

Together, they tugged and pulled, mouths locked, tongues tasting, and fingers exploring, until Marci finally lowered Tessa to the heap of clothes now mounded on the rock floor.

She hovered above Tessa, watching her, almost memorizing her, while she gently pushed her legs apart and teased her opening.

Tessa arched and splayed her fingers around the back of Marci's neck, pulling her lower. "Do it. Please."

With a moan, Marci pushed inside her.

Tessa whimpered and the sound encouraged Marci to go faster. She bucked into her, driving her fingers deeper with every stroke. Her body arched with every hitch of her hips, her mouth latched onto Tessa's lips, until they both came to the sound of their own erotic releases.

Marci rolled onto her side next to Tessa, gathering her breath, and stared at the ceiling of the cave. She thought of something her grandmother used to say.

Everything happens for a reason.

It had always seemed like such a clichéd thing to say. Everyone used that exact phrase. But for some reason, she now wondered if it was true. Did everything happen for a reason? Like a trail of bad luck all leading to something great? Whatever could have been the reason for the hell she'd been put through the last year? Whatever reason could there be to have the floor of her world jerked out from under her?

For this? For this time with Tessa? A woman who seemed to see this magnificent world almost exactly how Marci saw it? Beautiful and amazing and worth exploring?

Would Tessa laugh if she knew this was the only place where she truly felt more herself anymore? When her feet were on earth. When she was exploring.

The exact way she had found this waterfall and the space behind it. Exploring. Licking her wounds in private after coming back to this beautiful mountain with her tail between her legs. When she'd been at her lowest.

When she'd truly felt like she would never be okay again, these woods made her feel like it was okay to not be okay. Not even her own mother could say the right things to make her feel better. She only wanted the best for her. She wanted Marci to stop hurting but wound up smothering Marci instead. The same as Wendy had done. As much as she wanted them to stop, to just shut up, to just let her figure it out, she sure loved them for the attempt.

But if everything happened for a reason, was this that reason?

For this minute in time? For these unforgettable moments with Tessa? A woman who had successfully, for the second week, taken away all thoughts of Ashley?

Even if she didn't know she'd had the power to do so.

Marci should tell her. She should thank her for helping make her day okay. For making it simply okay. For allowing her the opportunity to hear the sound of Tessa's shocked release of breath as she took in her surroundings. That sound. Of adoration for something created out of nothing more than stone and dirt. That sound had made her heart sputter.

She was suddenly thrilled that Ashley had never given her the chance to help her discover a love for the great outdoors. It couldn't have sounded or felt nearly as enticing as it had coming out of Tessa's mouth.

"If you're going to let her in here with us, you at least have to share her with me," Tessa whispered.

Marci turned to look at her. Tessa was so beautiful with her hair tousled, lips plump, eyes sparkling against the light filtering through the waterfall. Did she know? Did she know that she was stunning? That her love for nature only enhanced that beauty?

Ashley was the last person Marci wanted to talk to Tessa about. The last person she wanted inside this space with them. Anyone else. But not Ashley.

"She's gone."

"Good." Tessa rolled over and straddled her hips and once again, they rode the climatic waves of pleasure.

Chapter Eight

So?" Wendy popped a French fry in her mouth and eyed Marci. "How did the team leaders manage to stay alive after three weeks of having to report to you? You haven't called me once to tell me that my days were numbered. Kind of scares me how quiet you've been."

"You're now complaining because I haven't complained? That's a new one." Marci wiped her mouth, tossed the napkin beside her plate, and took a sip of Coke.

"Yeah. Weird, right?"

Marci shrugged. She couldn't tell Wendy that she'd take every contestant on every team bitching in her office if it meant she got to conclude the day with Tessa tucked beneath her.

She couldn't stop her mind from driving straight to Tessa. Every day. Every night. Every waking moment. It was disturbing and completely against her new way of life. To never think about another woman again.

"Besides Donna having a meltdown in my office during week one, they've all pretty much left me alone except to bring me their itineraries. And other than having to contact them with a few scheduling conflicts all has been quiet."

Wendy dipped another fry in ketchup. "Has it now?"

"Why exactly would I lie about your misfits bothering me?"

"Has one misfit bothered you? One in particular? Has she bothered you?" She gave a quick eyebrow wiggle.

Marci reached out and yanked the red-tipped fry from her grasp and popped it in her own mouth. "You are very nosy."

"And you didn't answer the question." Wendy reached for a new fry.

"I shouldn't have to answer nosy, non business related questions."

"Oh my God! You had sex with her again, didn't you?" Wendy's voice seemed to bounce around the room, and Marci gave an apologetic nod to the nearest couple, who gave her an uneasy smile in return.

"Do you have to include everyone else in my private life?" Marci took another sip of Coke. "*My* private life, let me repeat."

"Yeah. Yeah. Whatever. But you did, right?" Wendy scooted up to the table, completely dismissing an entire burger she was famished for only minutes ago. "This is awesome. Like, amazingly awesome. This is…this is epic!"

"How is that epic, nimrod?" Marci lowered her voice. "It's just sex. Simple sex."

"No, ma'am. You're so, so wrong. On every level of the sexual world, it's not simple."

"Okay. I don't know what you spiked that Coke with, but you're losing your mind over this sex thing."

"Don't you get it? It's not simple. And it's not just sex, either. It's repeats." Wendy tapped her finger on the table as if that would drive her point home. "You never go back for repeats. Not since that witch rode off on her broomstick with your heart spitting out trails of blood like tattered ribbons."

Marci exaggerated a sigh. "Lord, here we go again."

"I'm being serious, Marci."

"Don't start, Wendy. I mean it. Don't start."

She was so sick of Wendy's wishful thinking that she was going to miraculously find someone to live happily ever after with.

There was no fucking happy ever after for her. That dream had been burned. Literally. She'd even tossed in the bedsheets that Ashley and her twat had fucked on. Burned. In a blazing glory in her firepit, in her backyard, at her own house, that soon would be gone, just like her future.

That dream had gone up in the same smoke created from burning their wedding pictures. Whatever clothes Ashley hadn't taken. Everything, right down to the trinkets they'd gotten on a road trip that had taken Marci three months to talk her into. The vacation she'd had to bribe her into, actually. One of those little road trips had cost her a brand new dining room set.

All of it. Gone. It was gone and she had no desire to revisit that kind of pain ever again. Why couldn't Wendy understand that? What did Marci have to do to make her see that she didn't and wouldn't have that kind of love in her life again? Ever.

"No, *you* stop!" Wendy's harsh voice pulled Marci's gaze up to meet hers. "That bitch did not break you. Do you understand me? She did *not* break you, and you need to stop acting like she got the last laugh."

The quiver in Wendy's voice made Marci reach for her. "Wendy."

Wendy snapped her hand back. "Don't Wendy me. I'm serious. I miss my best friend, dammit! The full of life, spontaneous, lover of this world, best friend. And if I have to verbally abuse you every day, I won't stop fighting until I peel back every single layer that loser burned on her way out the door, to find the real you. The old Marci. My Marci." She dramatically balled up her napkin and threw it at Marci, her bottom lip poked out, then she reached over, plucked Marci's napkin off the table, and threw that one at her, too.

Marci couldn't help it. She laughed. The sound started as a snicker and soon turned into both of them howling until Wendy snorted like a pig, a sound she only made when her whole body was invested in the laughter, and then they started laughing all over again.

It felt good to laugh. It felt even better to mean it.

She loved Wendy. Truly loved her. She was there when everyone else wasn't. She was Marci's shoulder when she had no one else to turn to. She was her sounding board when Marci felt like she was at the end of her rope.

But through it all, Wendy had still held strong to her hatred for Ashley. No matter how much she loved Marci, she couldn't, and wouldn't, accept the love of Marci's life. Yes, the very one who tilted her world off its axis, exactly as Wendy had predicted. She'd torn Marci's heart in half, exactly as Wendy said she would.

That might have been one of the hardest things she had to face. Wendy. She'd ignored all of those warnings. When Wendy wanted nothing but the best for her, she'd pushed her away. For Ashley. And not once since Marci had returned had she uttered those words: I told you so.

Eventually, she would. Marci knew her best friend better than that. Those words were coming.

"Feel better?" Marci dropped the napkins in the middle of the table.

"No!" Wendy shrugged and her expression softened. "Maybe."

"You know I'll be okay, don't you?" Marci leaned over and forced Wendy to look at her. "I'll be okay. I promise. It's just taking me a minute to breathe, that's all."

Wendy cocked her head and looked away. "Well, I wish you'd hurry. I've been working hard to help you get yourself back, to help you find yourself again, but you haven't even noticed."

"What do you mean I haven't noticed?"

"Trust me, you haven't noticed a single thing going on around you."

"I do notice, Wendy. And you know I love you, but you don't get to decide when I have to be okay. Let me do things my way. I'll find my way back, I promise."

Wendy watched her for several moments. Something in her eyes told Marci that she had indeed missed something. That there was something more than these heart-to-hearts over Ashley.

What that was, she wouldn't drag out of Wendy unless she was good and ready to reveal that information.

"I'm holding you to that promise." Wendy leaned in. "That cooty licker shouldn't get the pleasure of thinking she broke you."

Marci snickered. "You're a cooty licker, too, ya know?"

"She doesn't get to win, Marci. Not with you." Wendy shook her head and leaned back heavily in her chair. "Not with you."

Marci wished Wendy could just leave well enough alone, but the fact was, Wendy didn't know the meaning of letting bygones be bygones. This wasn't her fight. Wasn't her life. Wasn't her broken heart. Yet Wendy loved her enough to think they were.

Truth be told, there was nothing wrong with the way Marci was handling her separation.

Fucking and walking away. What was so horrible about that? Okay, so she was fucking and not walking away from Tessa, but that was only because she was easy access for the time being. And what was wrong with a little easy fun? They both knew when this game was over, win or lose, so was their time together.

"So, on a lighter note. Tessa's clients invited us to a party slash bonfire tonight. Did you get my email?" Marci hoped to change the subject once and for all.

"Yes. But do you think it's a wise choice for the boss to party with a crew? Would that show partiality to one team? One team in particular."

Marci shrugged. "I don't think it's wise to turn down a client invitation at all. You started this thing to draw business your way, right? To staff the additional resort once construction is complete. No better way to make a lasting impression than to show up for them."

"You started this, not me."

"Me? For sure you added too much spike to your Coke. You know I don't even like people, so there's no way in hell I would tell you that this contest was a good idea. Quite the opposite, actually."

Wendy dipped another fry and once again, Marci had a feeling she was missing an important piece of a puzzle. A puzzle she didn't even know she was working.

"I'm actually heading there when I finish this burger. Just come with me."

"If I'm going, I should probably show up without you considering the sideshow you have going on." Wendy winked.

"Then show up late, leave early. That should be good enough. Besides, you know you don't want to miss an all-lesbian party. It's not in your mental control to skip out."

Wendy seemed to mull over the idea even though a smirk lingered on her lips. "I guess you're right. If it was one of the other crews inviting me, I'd feel obligated to attend. So yeah. I'll be there. For just a little while."

"I bet you will." Marci winked as Wendy picked her burger up and bit off a huge chunk.

❖

Tessa checked the contents of the liquor cabinet one last time before she moved back into the throng of the party. At the rate these women were going, they would run out of booze long before they passed out.

She'd never seen anyone besides Monty who could actually drink like a fish and still walk a steady line. Her sister proudly took that ability to epic proportions.

She scanned the room and found Marci locked in a conversation with the bartender, hopefully to instruct the woman to start spiking the liquor with water. The poor woman had been pouring drinks all night. Had begun her night with colorful mixed drinks and was now flat-out pouring shots, regardless of what the women ordered. It appeared they could no longer tell the difference between a shot glass or a champagne flute.

When were these women going to start dropping out of the drinking race? How much longer could they hold out like this?

"Hey, sexy. Are you ever going to slow down?" Camille, her newest client, cooed from behind her. "We didn't invite you to this party so you could work all night."

Tessa turned around and found her personal space had been completely invaded. Again. Camille didn't have a clue what personal territory meant. Or didn't care. Which was more likely the case.

But she sure was a hottie. A boxer with numerous trophies, according to her endless conversations all night long that centered around her accomplishments.

Right now, she towered above Tessa by a good six inches, and damn, she smelled good.

Problem was, she'd been following Tessa around for hours, licking her lips in blatant invitation, undeterred by Tessa's one-line answers and quick dismissals. As hot as she was, as much fun as their rough sex could be, she absolutely detested a woman who didn't take no for an answer.

Because once she'd said no, she damn well meant it.

And she'd meant it when she said it four hours ago, three, two, and one hour ago, but she especially meant it fifteen minutes ago after she watched Marci walk through the front door.

Now those seductive pleas were getting on her ever-loving last nerve.

"You're my client. It's my job to work for you all night." Tessa stepped around her.

Camille gently cuffed her upper arm and stopped her forward progress. "Please stop and come hang with me. I've been begging all night."

Tessa gave her the sweetest smile she still possessed when she could feel her fangs and claws ready for action. "Yes, ma'am, you have. And I've been turning you down all night. Because I have a job to do."

Tessa resisted the urge to tell her that the real reason was standing across the room. That if luck was on her side she was going to be flat on her back with Marci hovering above her, inside her, when these bitches finally passed the hell out.

"If only I thought you meant no." Camille pulled Tessa to her chest and gave a devious smile.

"Camille?" Seth interrupted them. "Someone in the back needs you immediately."

Camille never took her sights off of Tessa. Her face remained calm as she stared down over her, her lips merely inches away. "Tell them I'm busy with far more important matters."

"They said it was very important. They used the word urgent, actually."

Camille groaned and released her tight hold on Tessa's arm. "I'll be right back, beautiful."

Seth bared his teeth as he watched her walk away. "If that woman didn't have the power to make us lose this game, or the muscles to punch my pretty face in, I'd whack her in the flipping head with a liquor bottle." His gaze swung back to Tessa. "You need to get your little ass on out of here, missy. She means to get right in your pants and you might not get a say-so in the decision."

"She's just drunk. They fall faster when they're intoxicated. So tell the bartender to start doubling those shots until she face-plants." Tessa patted his arm to assure him she wasn't concerned, although if Camille didn't pass out soon, she might have to consider plan B because she always had a say-so in who got around the bases with her, and she one hundred percent had a say in who got in her pants. "Just make sure when she starts puking, she does it over the hardwood floor please."

She picked up empty beer bottles from the coffee table while he huffed and beelined for the bartender. Tessa had only been half kidding. But seeing as he took her seriously, she wasn't kidding anymore. Drunken face-plants would have to do for the handsy one tonight. No way in hell would Tessa allow that woman to hurt their chances of getting every point out of Camille's entourage. She'd come too far to let tequila stand in her way.

For another thirty minutes, the party continued without a hitch. Women danced in the great room. Music screamed through the house. A bonfire blazed in the backyard. And everyone was laughing and smiling and having the time of their life, even if they were all enhanced by alcohol.

Until.

"I'm back, sexy." Camille captured Tessa from behind and ground her hips hard into Tessa's ass. "Did you miss me?"

"Ah, Camille." Tessa tried to squirm out of her tight hold. "Is everything okay with your friend?"

"Yes. She's a wimp and can't hang with the big dogs." Camille ground into her again. "Her wife put her to bed where said wimps belong. Speaking of beds. How about we go find one." She pushed Tessa's hair to the side and bit the flesh just below her ear.

"Ouch!" Tessa jerked forward and pulled herself free of those clutching hands. "Rough, much?" She rubbed the spot on her neck and gave Camille a hard glare.

"I can tell you like it rough." Camille licked her lips and stepped forward. "I like to give it rough. And I can't wait to give it to you rough."

Tessa stepped back and looked across the room. She found Marci staring at her, a look of pure anger dominating her expression.

Marci took a deep breath. It was all she could do not to charge across the room and lay the inconsiderate bitch out.

She'd been watching the altercation for too long, getting more and more jealous by the minute. Although jealous was a strong word for someone who didn't get jealous.

Whatever she was feeling, it was in high gear right now as she watched Tessa rub her neck, apparent pain and shock on her gorgeous face, doing all she could do, with utmost consideration, to just say no.

But running to her aid or interfering would be Tessa's downfall. And whatever happened from that point on would all be blamed on Marci. If Tessa lost this round in the game, it would be Marci's fault. If Marci did nothing, it would still be her fault for watching and not intervening. And if Tessa gave in and fucked that bitch, it would be her undoing.

Not tonight. Not while so many wicked thoughts were scampering through her mind. Not while she needed Tessa all to herself tonight.

Tonight, Tessa would be hers and hers alone.

As soon as she figured out how to put an end to this unfolding drama, that is. Without making an ass of herself, embarrassing Tessa, or having to sport an orange jumpsuit in the detention center at the base of the mountain.

Camille pulled Tessa to her once again, and Marci's grip tightened around her glass.

She had to do something. She couldn't sit back and watch this another second.

With a little more force than she meant, Marci slammed her glass down on the mantle and started across the room, glad that Wendy had come and gone and couldn't talk her out of a possible bad decision. And she had a sneaky suspicion she was about to make a very bad decision.

Tessa attempted to keep the polite smile on her face as Camille tightened the grip around her arm. No one would make her lose her composure when her future, possibly the future of her entire crew, was riding on her being able to keep her temper in check.

However, she'd had enough. Actually, she'd had enough hours ago. Had enough of having a grown woman paw at her all night. Having to run like Penelope from Pepé Le Pew. And honestly, not being heard the first five hundred times she'd made it clear that she wasn't interested, even though in any other setting, she could have possibly been.

And finally, because Marci was across the room, watching her most of the night with those rich brown eyes, silently promising erotic endings to an otherwise hectic weekend.

And right now, Marci was making her way across the room wearing an aggravated expression.

Before Marci could act like a brazen hero, Tessa needed to put a halt to this disaster in the making.

She gave in to Camille's tug and pretended to step into a friendly hug, even though the grip on her arm remained tight and demanding.

With her heart hammering, she pressed her lips against Camille's ear. "I need you to nod like we're solving a private business matter. Do you understand, Camille?"

Camille gave a single nod.

"Let me be perfectly clear. I never mix fucking with business. Especially when my future is on the line. Especially when I have a crew looking up to me and depending on me to be on my best behavior. Nod, Camille. And smile."

Once again, Camille gave a nod.

"Under any other circumstances, I would have already pushed you down to your knees and ridden your tongue like a vibrator. But this is business, and you have been completely disrespectful to me, my crew, and more importantly, to yourself, all night. So unless you want me to drop-kick your drunk ass in front of God and everyone else in this room, I suggest you take yourself up those stairs and tuck it into bed. Nod, Camille."

This time, Camille's nod was tight and quick.

"And tomorrow, when you're sitting down with your scorecard, I suggest your revenge be targeted on me. Not my crew. They did nothing wrong and your points should, and better, reflect the great work they have done for you all weekend. Nod."

Once again, Camille gave a tight nod.

"Now, I'm going to pull away, and you're going to let go of me, then we are going to shake hands like grown adults and walk away." Tessa ground her teeth together and pushed her lips harder against Camille's ear. "One last thing, dipshit. No *always* means no."

Camille loosened the grip on Tessa's arm and her posture shrank.

Tessa stepped back, smile fastened to her lips like a window cling.

She turned to walk away and found Marci only feet away, dark expression on her face, feet hip-width apart, standing tall and threatening.

Her insides clamped down tight at the clear protective posture.

Camille stormed off and Tessa had a heavy pit in her stomach. Tomorrow, before Camille left this lodge, she was going to take it out on Tessa. That fact made her heart heavy yet there was nothing she could do to alter the revenge that Camille would surely dish out while scoring this entire team.

Seth charged up beside Marci. "Please get her the hell out of here before that buffoon changes her mind and comes back!"

Marci followed Camille's departure before her features softened and she looked down at Tessa.

"Absolutely."

Thirty minutes later, Tessa landed on her back in the middle of Marci's bed. Exactly where she wanted to be.

Chapter Nine

Tessa immediately felt the weight pinning her leg down as she slowly lifted out of sleep. Marci's weight. One arm rested across her stomach. The other was tucked under Tessa's head. She was normally claustrophobic when it came to things that restricted her movement. This was different. This time the confinement was sensual and comforting.

She cracked an eye open to find dim light filtering through the window. The morning was awakening beyond the panes, silhouetting the trees in the distance.

She'd fallen asleep in Marci's bed. Passed out was more like it.

She couldn't remember the last time she'd done that. Had a sleepover. Fell asleep with a woman beside her. In their bed. Years, no doubt.

Not that she didn't believe in love or commitment. She just didn't believe in it for herself. Possibly because she'd planned one too many weddings for people who had already vowed their love, life, and commitments to someone before. Sometimes several times before.

Those ceremonies, time and time again, left her just a little more bitter. A little more sold on the fact that genuine love might never be possible for her. Was true love so rare? Was it that hard to cling to? To find? Was it like a needle in that haystack, forcing people to give up the needle and settle for the hay?

According to her sister's wedding planning schedule, the one Tessa had helped finalize before she left, the one that listed plans for second and third marriages, she had proof that love was indeed rare.

When, if, she ever found love and promised herself to another forever, she was going to mean it. But for now, being single, and being okay with being single, was far easier than winding up with multiple engagement rings in her jewelry box.

But right now, love, relationships, or sleepovers were the furthest things from her mind. She had a future ahead of her. The one she'd been reaching for for far too long. And depending on her run in this game, and Camille's memory of last night, she could easily achieve that goal. But she needed to do it with a clear head. Every minute she spent with Marci, in or out of her bed, was chipping away at the valuable time she could be spending on her clients. Planning for the next clients.

Marci opened her eyes to find Tessa staring out the window. She was stunning with her tousled hair framing her face. How was she still single? Was she, in fact, single? Why hadn't she thought to ask before now? How had she not thought to consider that until now? Cheaters were at the top of her thought process now. The very thing she vowed to avoid by fucking all the people passing through. So how in the world had that one simple question dodged her lips?

She'd awoken several times during the night to the heat of Tessa snuggled into her, and it felt strange. She wasn't used to sharing her bed all night. And if she had to be honest, Ashley wasn't the cuddle type, preferring her side of their king-size bed to be all hers. Hell, until Ashley, she'd rarely shared a bed with anyone else at all.

Sharing that space with Tessa had been a welcoming comfort. One she didn't know she missed until now. The realization gave her solace. Likely, it shouldn't. But it did.

"Are you having a mental conversation with the trees?" Marci snuggled her face into the crook of Tessa's neck and pressed her lips against the steady pulse.

Tessa hummed and angled her head back.

It was incredible how responsive she was to Marci's touch. How her body arched and bowed with every kiss. How she cocooned Marci in her grasp while her fingers were buried deep, like she was holding on to every minute of their time.

Those little things made Marci feel important. Wanted. Even needed. Like her actions were valued and every caress of exploration had reached Tessa's soul. Sure, she was overthinking, but she couldn't shake the feeling.

"Yes. I'm asking them to give me energy since it was all consumed last night," Tessa whispered.

Marci wrapped her free arm around Tessa's hip, pulled her closer, and tucked the length of her beneath her own. "That's a perfect request." She rolled on top and gently pushed her legs open. "You're going to need lots more energy."

Tessa instinctively thrust upward and she draped her arms around Marci's neck. "Not this time, stud. I am absolutely depleted of muscle control." She leaned forward and captured Marci's lips in complete mockery of her words.

Marci ground into her, rotating her hips, driving Tessa against the mattress. "Is this a case of no always means no? Which was hot as hell listening to you spit those words out to a freaking trophied boxer, by the way." She drove down harder. "Unlike her, should I be a gentleman and stop?"

"God no." Tessa fisted her fingers into Marci's hair and pulled her back down. "Don't stop."

Marci was positive last night would have filled her appetite for Tessa. She was incredibly wrong. Even now, barely any sleep, her body splendidly sore from so much sex, her insides throbbed for more.

It helped that Tessa seemed just as hungry, no matter what her words said.

Marci pushed her hand between them, seeking that warm, wet opening, and gently eased inside.

Tessa ground her head into the pillow, her fingers tightening in Marci's hair, a moan escaping those plump lips.

This, this reaction, as if Marci had found that sexual center that operated all of her senses, amazed her. She'd never had sex with someone who responded to every touch, every kiss, and every buck of her hips. Not anyone who had seemed genuine, anyway. It was addicting. She wanted to touch her everywhere. Wanted to kiss her longer. Wanted to fuck her harder. Just to hear those cries of release.

Tessa's body froze in an arch, and then she clutched at Marci, bucking up to meet her thrusts.

Marci continued to fuck her, inhaling those musical sounds of satisfaction, until Tessa sagged beneath her.

"No more," Tessa managed. "I mean it. My body can't take anymore."

Tessa was aware that her chest was rising and falling. That Marci fit perfectly along her body. That she was breathing. Alive. But every nerve in her body felt nothing more than prickly tingles to tell her she might still have sensation in her limbs after all.

She was in complete awe that her body was still capable of functioning, let alone able to produce another toe curling orgasm. So much sex. Heaven help her, so much sex had happened in this bed all night. And if Marci so much as touched her, her body ignited with need as if she hadn't been fucked in years.

It was insane. How was she doing it? How was she able to awaken her needs so quickly after awakening them hour after hour?

Sure, she'd had fantastic lovers. But none as intuitive as Marci. She was perfect, in fact. Rough, easy, slow, fast, as if she could read Tessa's every desire. As if her only goal was to satisfy those desires. She'd never had someone so in tune with her. Anyone who seemed to care to be in tune with her.

Marci rolled onto her side and stared over at Tessa. "Do you practice witchcraft?"

Tessa eyed her suspiciously. "I wish. I would wiggle my nose or point a wand and fix the whole world."

"Hmm. Then do you morph into wolf form on the full moon?"

Intrigued with the line of questions, Tessa rolled onto her side to face Marci. "Not just any wolf. A dire wolf. Nymeria is my name because I am a warrior queen."

"She's a *Game of Thrones* fanatic. Cute." Marci grinned and Tessa resisted kissing her. Kissing would lead her right back to another orgasm, and she was quite certain her body would self-destruct the next time.

"Do you swallow your fingernails, maybe?"

"Gross. No."

"Sniff people's feet?"

"Eww. No!" Tessa laughed and her insides squeezed in protest. Her body had never quite responded so much. "What the hell are you getting at, freak?"

"Well, it's not like you're a hag or anything. But you're single. For a reason." Marci trailed a finger along her ribcage, igniting a path of heat. "You *are* single. Right?"

Tessa could hear the plea, and the mistrust, in her question. It made her sad. Marci was living proof that love could be destroyed in the blink of an eye. Someone had cheated on her. Someone she loved. Trusted. They had stabbed that knife deep.

"Completely single. Not partially. Not halfway. Not even an ex looking to get back together, kind of single." Tessa took her hand and placed it between them, mainly because those soft caresses were heating her skin all over again. "Tell me about her. Your cheating ex."

Marci briefly looked away but not before Tessa caught the light of pain in her eyes. Whatever happened, she'd never seen it coming. The sucker punch.

"Instead, why don't you tell me how long you've been a wedding planner."

"Since potty training, I think?" Tessa grinned. "My mom passed down the trait to me and my big sister, Michelle."

"Only one sibling?"

"Two. I have a half sister much younger than me. Monty. She is the polar opposite of me and Michelle. You?"

"Only child. Only grandchild. Both my mom and dad were only children and grandchildren. Giving up at one seems to run in the family." Marci played with Tessa's fingers.

"Count yourself lucky. I spend most of my time making Michelle's dreams come true at our, her, venue and keeping Monty out of jail."

"Ah. A troublemaking black sheep?"

"Oh no. She's actually amazing. Great friend. Fantastic sister. Chef at a five-star restaurant. Worked hard to gain her position. Volunteers at the homeless shelter once a month. Very dependable. Adores her family. Adored by the community. Thinks I walk on water, poor thing. Pays her own bills. Stunning apartment overlooking the city. Extremely mature in most ways."

"I hear a huge but coming."

"She can't keep her hands off married women to save her ass from a beat down."

Tessa hadn't meant to make light of the facts about her little sister. Truth was, her behavior was disgusting. It was disturbing. But no matter how many times she scolded her, or even begged her to stop the bullshit, Monty was a grown adult and Tessa couldn't make her behave.

"Not cool," Marci said.

"Not cool at all. I love her to death. Would protect her until my dying breath. But that bad habit drives me to cuss. It disappoints me, ya know?"

Marci nodded, and Tessa could tell the subject was hitting too close to home.

"Your turn. Tell me about her."

"Not much to tell. She cheated. I went in one direction. She went in another. End of story."

"That simple, huh?"

"That simple."

"And did she admit why she did such an ugly thing to you?"

"I didn't give her a chance. There wasn't a single excuse that would change the outcome."

"The outcome didn't have to change to get that answer. Don't you think you deserved that answer?"

"I deserved to not be cheated on. So I didn't give a shit what excuse she had."

"That would explain your hostility and mistrust."

"How so?"

"You haven't found your closure. Haven't come to grips with what she did. You still don't know what made her stoop so low."

"Oh, I got plenty of closure. I burned everything she left behind. Packed my shit, put my house on the market, and came home."

"That's not closure. That's angry mode. That's robotically shifting into self-defense."

"What else was I supposed to do? Thank her for the porn show, then go back to work as if my whole world wasn't crumbling around me?"

"Absolutely not."

"Then what was I supposed to do?"

Tessa shrugged. "I'm not an expert on cheaters, nor am I a cheater. But you're going to run across her again someday if you're lucky. Ask her why. Your closure will be in her answer. I promise. And then you'll be free of your own chains."

Marci considered her words. Had she been robotic? Too fast to ship out? Too quick to run? Should she have given Ashley the chance to explain, even if the answer wouldn't, couldn't, change the ending? Did she even care why anymore? Was her need to fuck and walk away now the chain still binding her to Ashley?

What exactly would have given her closure? Hearing the why? Was there any answer that might have mattered? No. She couldn't think of anything that would have made the pain stop. Nothing Ashley could have said would have taken away the fact that the world as she knew it was over. Just like that. All gone.

"Did you know the person she cheated with?"

"No. Some twat much younger than her. Caught them in the act. In my fucking house. In my fucking bed."

"Ouch. That punch hurt. What a douche."

"That she fucked someone or that she did it under our roof."

"All of the above. But the bed is personal. If someone ever cheated on me in my own bed, I would be severely tempted to burn them alive in it. Don't fuck with my bed."

Marci snickered. "I burned the sheets and sold the bed."

"Did you stuff her body in the mattress?" Tessa added a playful smile.

"Nah. But the thought of stuffing that other bitch in it did cross my mind." Marci trailed a line over the curve of Tessa's hip, already tired of talking about Ashley. Wendy had worn that subject out.

"Oh no. It wasn't the other woman's fault. Never blame the wrong person. Your wife did this to you. Not her young little twat, as you called her."

"It's hard not to blame them both."

"I'm sorry she did that to you. That had to be pretty rough. How long were you together?"

"Eleven years. Married nine of them."

"That's a long time considering most couples don't make it five. You must have really loved her."

"Let's talk about something else. Or just whimper. That sounds much better." Marci leaned down and captured a nipple between her lips and gave a light suckle.

Tessa rolled over with a moan and squirmed against the mattress, her hips lifting slightly off the mattress. "You didn't say her name."

Marci leaned up to look at her. Was she serious? "You want to know her name? Now?"

"Yes. Say her name." Tessa pushed Marci's hand between her legs and ground against it.

Marci teased her wet opening and then eased her fingers inside, hoping she would forget her request. She was sick to death of talking about a dead subject.

Tessa hissed and matched her thrusts. "Say it, Marci."

"Ashley. Dammit."

"Well, remember this, Miss Marci. Ashley only got a piece of you." She covered Marci's hand with her own and pushed her in deeper. "Your best revenge is to make sure it wasn't the best piece."

Out of every grueling conversation with Wendy, not a single sentence had struck a chord the way Tessa's just had. She was so right. Ashley might have put a dent in her, but she didn't break her. Dammit. She wasn't broken. And how true those words were. It was up to her to get back on track, to put the ugly past behind her, and to give all of herself to the next person in line.

She rolled on top of Tessa, silenced her with a hard kiss, then bucked inside her.

An hour later, Tessa finally crawled out of the bed. She was in desperate need of a shower. Her body was so sore it made her groan. Pain that banked on pure satisfaction or a freight train disaster. The way her muscles ached, she wasn't so sure anymore. She had no clue that much bliss could be so tense. Wow. So. Much. Sex. She was positive her whole lifespan of orgasms couldn't match this single night. Including, but not limited to, her own masturbation.

Her head swam and she struggled to remember the last time she'd eaten. Or drank. Many hours ago, for sure.

A cup of coffee would help before she headed to the lodge to start the cleaning and restocking phase. Camille and her rowdy friends would be departing soon. Their transportation was due early this morning. Her and her crew's scorecards would be turned in to Wendy shortly before their flight left, as Wendy was the last line of communication and saw each set of clients off at the airport. Within a few hours, Tessa would get the dreaded news.

Tessa's private outburst could have possibly cost her team the win. Hell, if Camille wanted to get downright nasty about being put in her place, if only she and Tessa and Marci had heard all of it, she and her crew could be headed home by nightfall.

The thought made her sad. And angry. She'd worked so hard. Her crew had been amazing every step of the way. No way Camille could be the petty, immature, drunken ending none of them deserved.

"Where do you think you're going?" Marci reached for her.

"I need coffee, a shower, and more coffee before I head back up to the lodge to see what kind of damage awaits me." Tessa dodged the outstretched hand and searched the bedroom floor for her clothes, tugged off and tossed away in the rushed throes of lust. "And I think I need to squeeze food in there somewhere. I can't tell if I'm famished or I've pulled a muscle." She tossed Marci a teasing grin.

"Grab a shower here." Marci scooted off the bed and pulled Tessa against her chest. "I'll get us some coffee started. I can even whip up a mean omelet."

"Mmm. That sounds great." Tessa draped her arms around Marci's neck, completely aware of the quickening in her gut.

Not from the mention of food. Or coffee. Not from hunger. Not from too many sexual abdominal crunches.

She liked Marci. That was the problem. That was the familiar stirring. She liked Marci's personality. Loved that she loved the great outdoors as much as she did. Hated that she liked and loved those things about her. She absolutely shouldn't.

But this wouldn't last much longer, Tessa reminded herself.

The game was nearing an end. Too close to the end, if Camille had anything to do with it. Regardless, once this contest was over, whether that be in a few hours or the next few weeks, her time with Marci would be over.

Marci, and these little stolen moments of sexual magic, couldn't be a roadblock on her path to success. Actually, Tessa wouldn't allow her to be. As much fun as this was, nothing and no one would stand in her way.

"Thanks. But I need to get back to my cabin so Seth can give me the lowdown on last night's adventures."

"You sure?" Marci tucked a strand of hair behind her ear. "I'm positive I can prove you wrong on the pulled muscle theory."

Tessa playfully pushed against her. "I'm sure. But thanks for the offer. If I'm still a participant by the end of the day, a rain check will be necessary, however."

Tessa regretted the words as soon as they left her lips. This needed to stop. Not because it was against any rules. Simply because Tessa was going to get in her own way if she wasn't careful.

No. This had to stop. Very soon. Very, very soon. And the way Marci was devouring her with those chocolate eyes, she might never escape this paradise.

Marci gave a nod. "In that case, I'll go throw myself in the shower. Have a great day." She turned and headed for the bathroom.

Tessa watched her retreating naked form, second-guessing her decision to shower in her own cabin. Marci had proven she was pretty good on her knees.

She blinked at the thought and quickly headed for the front door. The cold air outside would help cool down the snaking desire to join Marci.

Her coat was tossed over a chair in Marci's office so she ducked in to grab it and noticed a file in the center of the desk. Her name was handwritten on the tab.

Curiosity won over being respectful of someone else's privacy so she plucked it off the desk and flipped the cover open.

A five-by-seven picture of her was taped to the inside. The very one on the venue website that was snuggled right beside Michelle's.

Tessa Dalton. Peoria, Arizona. Wedding Planner. Group Leader.

Tessa felt her breath snag in her throat as she read the adjoining page. Her age. Her experiences. The name and address of the venue. What day she had been accepted to the contest. How she was chosen to be the group leader. All listed in the different blocks on a form letter.

"What the fuck," Tessa whispered, anger crawling through her like slow rolling fog.

How long had Marci had this file? Before the contest? After?

Had she known who Tessa was as soon as she stepped into that bar?

Too many questions filtered through her mind.

She charged back to the bathroom, unclear what she wanted to say. Or what she wanted to ask. She only knew that she couldn't leave without getting an answer.

Steam filled the room as she yanked open the sliding doors and thrust the file forward.

"Changed your mind?" Marci wiped water from her face and looked down at Tessa.

Her joking smile melted from her lips as she focused on the file.

"How long have you had this? Did you know who I was before I got here? Did you know who I was when you fucked me all night?" Tessa shoved the folder closer.

"Yes. No. Wait. No!" Marci stumbled over her words as Tessa backed away, fuming.

"Did you or did you not have this folder before this contest began? Fucking yes or no!"

"Yes, but I—"

"You accused me of trying to fuck my way to the finish line, Marci. And you meant it. And yet *you* are the one who knew exactly who I was?" Tessa took another step back, conflicted between the need to hear Marci's response and the fear of hearing a lie. "You are a twisted mental case. And a dirty sleazebag. A genuine, fucking class A dirty sleazebag." She dropped the file on the floor. "Stay the hell away from me. I mean it."

Tessa charged from the room. She grabbed her coat and jerked open the front door just as she heard footsteps pounding from the bedroom.

She slammed the door behind her, angry tears threatening, though she didn't know why.

Marci was nothing to her. Nothing more than a release of pent up energy created from this chaotic game. The game that could deliver her a future she envisioned long before this contest. The future she'd been dreaming of for so long.

So why was she on the verge of mad crying? Because Marci decided to throw a twist in the contest by fucking one of the contestants? What exactly was her plan for that? Why did Tessa give a shit at all? And why hadn't she practiced what she'd preached only hours ago? Why hadn't she listened to Marci's answer?

Because she was afraid there was a logical explanation, that's why.

Because Marci was right. The excuses couldn't change the ending.

Her ending, if Camille hadn't sabotaged it, didn't include Marci Jones or her ability to give multiple orgasms.

This was for the best. This was exactly what Tessa wanted. A reason not to look back. A reason to stay far away from Marci.

She was nothing more than a distraction.

A distraction she wouldn't be allowing again.

CHAPTER TEN

Marci plopped down in the chair across from Wendy's desk. She hadn't planned on driving down to the resort to vent or whine or bitch, but after four days of trying to contact Tessa, she needed to get the hell out of that cabin.

The walls were closing in on her. Minute by minute, her thoughts were consumed with the need to explain herself. To make Tessa listen.

Tessa wouldn't answer her texts. Wouldn't answer phone calls. And going to her cabin was completely out of the question. That was one line she wouldn't cross. She wouldn't involve Tessa's crew in personal drama. Although, she'd come very close.

She was hoping to intercept Tessa during one of her morning walks, or even her ritual evening strolls, but even those had vanished. She'd had nothing. Not a single glimpse of her unless it was darting to the Jeep. Hell, she'd even sent Seth to Marci's cabin with their itinerary for the new clients again instead of coming herself. She wanted to congratulate her on winning top points again when she truly thought Camille was going to seek revenge in the most distasteful way. Yet she hadn't. She and her posse had raved about the crew, how professional they were, and how fortunate they were to have gotten Tessa's crew for their vacation.

Marci had been tempted to ask Seth about her. Tempted to beg him to make Tessa return her phone calls. Wouldn't that have been mature? No, she wouldn't have looked like a crazy person at all.

"Man, if you don't look like shit." Wendy turned away from her computer and arched a brow. "I take it she still won't speak to you?"

"Not even a text." Marci forked her fingers through her hair and leaned back.

"I probably shouldn't be talking to you about this at all, since I'm basically her boss, but the fact is, if you had done your job like I asked you to to begin with, this whole fiasco could have been avoided. Going over those files was your only job." Wendy shrugged. "You only had one job."

"Thanks for the reminder, pal."

Wendy dismissed her sarcasm, turned back to her monitor, and clicked a button on the mouse. "You know I'm right."

"According to you, you're always right. Yet you still find the need to remind me."

"I have to remind you because you will sit right there and play the victim for the next hour if I let you."

"I'm not playing the victim."

Wendy turned in her chair and pushed the reading glasses on top of her head. "Then why are you sitting across from me with your bottom lip rolled out like a red carpet pretending that she doesn't have a legitimate reason to assume you're an ass?"

"I get it, Wendy. I know how it looked. I just wish she would give me the chance to explain."

"Kind of the way you gave her a chance to explain?"

Marci angled her head and stared hard at Wendy. "Damn. Drive the knife hard, won't you?"

Wendy's expression softened. "Marci, you know how desperate I am to see you back in the game, but maybe Tessa isn't the one you should have your sights set on." She leaned against the desk, her eyes so serious Marci had to look away.

It was true. She indeed had her focus set on someone. The wrong one. Tessa had a one-track mind. Her mind was set on this game. Winning. Set on her new career taking flight.

All of that was fine. She was great with Tessa's new career taking off. It wasn't like she was proposing a marriage.

She wanted Tessa to know she hadn't lied. It was important that Tessa knew the truth, that she wasn't playing some sick game.

"I don't have my sights set on Tessa. I just don't like her thinking I am a liar. Once I get that off my chest, all will be good and I can be free to move about the cabin."

"Okay. So write her a letter and have one of her crew give it to her. Case closed."

"A letter? Seriously? Please don't mock me." Marci felt the bite of her words. "We're not in grade school, Wendy. This isn't a check yes or no kind of problem solving issue."

"True." Wendy studied her for a few seconds, her brow creased in deep concentration. "Holy shit, you're smitten with her, aren't you?"

"Oh my God. Of course not." Marci threw her hands up and hoped the reaction appeared genuine.

Fact was, she didn't know what she was. Only that she was in turmoil because a beautiful woman wouldn't speak to her. A beautiful woman who she had so much in common with that it was like looking in a mirror sometimes.

And she wouldn't give Marci the time of day to defend herself. She wanted nothing more to do with Marci, no matter how glorious their time together had been.

It was downright unnerving and she couldn't think about anything else.

She had to talk to Tessa. Had to.

"Okay, so you don't like her. She doesn't like you. I don't see the problem."

"I simply want to tell her that she's wrong about me. I'm not a damn liar."

"In that case, you should run up to the lodge and say those exact words. Tell her she's wrong. Because telling a woman she's wrong always goes over well."

Marci felt a seed of hope. "She's up at the lodge?"

"Yep. All alone. Stocking for her next clients."

Marci slowly rose from the chair when her instincts were to race from the room and drive like a maniac all the way up the mountain.

"Think you could have told me that to begin with?"

"And miss all this important conversation and the chance to watch you squirm? No way."

"You're impossible." Marci scooted around the chair.

"One more thing," Wendy blurted.

Marci turned around but kept her motion for the door.

"When you see it, let me know."

"When I see what?" Marci gripped the doorframe to stop herself from running.

"Nothing. Go. Go tell her she's wrong."

Marci studied Wendy's serious expression, knowing she wouldn't pry anything else from her. So she turned and jogged down the hallway.

Finally, she would get to see Tessa.

Tessa stocked the last of the groceries in the pantry and stored the empty bags under the kitchen sink.

She had twenty-four hours before the new clients would arrive. A sweet couple who had been married over forty-nine years and wanted to celebrate the big five-oh anniversary with their children and grandchildren.

Tessa had thrown herself into their celebration, making sure everything would be perfect and sweet and unforgettable. They were the kind of people she strived to be. Finding the one. Not the second or third one. Holding on to the one. And cherishing every day they had together.

But they sure had set the bar high.

That's what this life was all about, right? Love, family, and sharing it to the end?

Well, everyone else's life, that is.

Right now, she just wanted to watch love from afar. Wanted to plan those weddings and events and keep pushing forward until someone rang the bell and named her the winner.

Then she was going to dive into the next step. The next step of becoming a world-renowned wedding planner. She wanted people to seek out her services far and wide. She wanted brides to plan their weddings around her calendar.

She could. She would. Become that person.

She'd worked too hard to be anything less.

Tessa sighed and looked around the kitchen, searching for anything she might have forgotten.

The rooms were stocked and ready. The pantry was full. The fridge was packed. The lodge was clean. There was absolutely nothing left for her to do. She was ready for them.

So why was she still standing here? She could be out hiking on this beautiful day. She could have gone into town for some shopping and dining with her crew. Or better, she could be curled up on the couch at the pond house reading a book and relaxing.

Except that place would only make her think of Marci. Would remind her how sexy she had been dropping to her knees at that very couch.

Right now, she didn't want to think about Marci. At all. She wanted to get on with this game, wanted to give everything she had, without a single distraction. And Marci was far too sexy of a distraction.

Of course, she was without willpower to stop the images of their time together from invading on their own. No matter what she was doing, Marci seemed to sneak in. It was aggravating and downright out of character.

She needed to get her shit back together.

But first she would have to admit to Marci that she'd overreacted. That she'd used a moment in time to be the catalyst for their ending. Not that they'd ever truly began.

Fact was, she'd been getting too close. Getting too comfortable. Enjoying Marci's company, all that amazing sex, far more than she should have.

She was in the middle of a contest. A contest she could bleed to win if she had to. There was no room for Marci. No room for anything other than her team and clients.

They were the ones who would help her get to the finish line. Not Marci.

And Marci deserved to hear those words from her. No more storming off. No more avoiding her phone calls or texts. It was time to face her and admit that what was happening between them had to end. Had already ended.

Footsteps sounded behind her, and Tessa spun around to find Marci standing entirely too close.

"Sorry. Didn't mean to scare you."

Tessa's heart thundered in her chest. Not from fright. But from being too close. Because Marci looked delicious in her faded jeans and black jacket. Because her lips looked inviting and Tessa had thought about sitting on them for days.

Fuck!

Tessa took in a deep breath in an attempt to calm her now frazzled nerves.

What was it about Marci that made Tessa's insides quiver at the simple sight of her?

"No problem. I was just getting ready to leave, actually. Was making sure I hadn't forgotten anything."

"Can we talk? Please? Since you won't take my calls?"

Those apologetic eyes bored through Tessa. They were sinfully sexy, and Tessa had to look away to keep her thoughts in check.

"Look, Marci. It's fine."

"No, it's not. Just let me say it, Tessa. Okay?"

Tessa nodded when all she really wanted to do was leave this house, leave Marci standing there, and go. Outside those doors was air. Right now, she was finding it hard to breathe. Right now, she just wanted to get naked, wanted Marci all over her, in her, and then she wanted to do it again.

"I know what it looked like. But I swear I never opened the file. I couldn't."

Tessa forced herself to look at Marci, knowing she should interrupt her, tell her that the truth didn't matter, that this, whatever this was, had to stop. It had to stop because she had a life to get to, a goal to reach, and Marci was only in her way.

"I saw your name. Saw you were from Peoria. Where my life with Ashley had been for eleven years." Marci looked down and kicked a spot on the floor. "So instead of doing my job, instead of not letting her get under my skin, I went to the bar to have a drink. Like a coward."

Marci took a shallow breath and barged right on. "I'm sick of being sick. I'm tired of being tired. I'm pissed that I'm always pissed. And when I'm with you, she loses her control of me."

Marci looked back up and it was all Tessa could do not to reach for her. She hated that Marci hadn't gotten her closure. Hated that someone had hurt her. Hated that the next woman in line would have to piece her back together. Hated more that she liked the idea of being that next woman.

It was a ridiculous thought. She didn't do relationships. Didn't want to be in one, let alone have to be the glue to fix some broken soul.

But for a minute, maybe five, she'd thought of being just that. Of being the woman who made Marci forget that a piece of shit had ripped apart her world. That a cheating piece of scum had rocked the foundation out from under her. And that when she was screaming Marci's name, that bitch was missing out. And somehow, Tessa knew that Ashley knew it too.

But that idea was far from the reality she had chosen for herself. She didn't have time to coddle Marci. Didn't have time to help find the pieces to Marci's broken life. And she sure as hell didn't have the need or even the time to put her back together.

Marci was watching her. Waiting for her response.

She had one. Only one. The very one she'd been thinking about for days now.

One that definitely wouldn't put Humpty Dumpty back together again.

"Take off your clothes, Marci."

Marci's brow arched for a split second before a smile snaked across her lips.

She stepped into Tessa and roughly captured her lips.

Tessa hummed and fisted her fingers into her hair before Marci pulled her down to the carpet.

This time, their sex was rough and needy. Almost angry and desperate.

And when Tessa fell back in a boneless heap, her insides still tight and pulsing, she knew she was in trouble.

She liked Marci. Too much. That was a fact. A horrible, horrible fact.

Marci could almost feel Tessa's mood shift as she stared up at the vaulted ceiling, her skin clammy and sweaty and still tingling everywhere Tessa had touched her.

How could Marci miss something she'd never had? How could she miss Tessa all the years she hadn't known her? They were perfect. And that was terrifying.

Tessa had a goal. Marci wasn't part of that plan.

And she didn't care.

Whatever time Tessa would give her, she was going to take.

And when this game was over, when Tessa had won this contest, Marci would figure out what to do then.

Because she knew beyond a shadow of a doubt, that was when the real missing Tessa would begin.

"Go out with me tonight." Marci rushed the words before she could change her mind.

"On a date?"

Marci rolled onto her side and trailed a path around those perfect breasts. "Yes. A real date."

"Marci, I don't think—"

Marci pushed her index finger against Tessa's lips to silence her. Mainly because she didn't want to be rejected. Not today. Today, she just wanted to forget that their end was in sight. That Tessa was going to say those words very soon. And if Tessa didn't, Marci would.

"Don't think. Just say yes."

Marci knew asking her out on a date was making a mistake. She'd been making mistakes from the second she turned around on a bar stool and found Tessa standing there.

She should have told her the truth. That they couldn't keep going. That this had been fun. A lot of fun. But she didn't trust women at all, and that might never change. Not anytime soon.

But damn if she could take it back. Hell, she wasn't even sure she wanted to take it back.

What harm could a few more weeks of sex be?

"Yes." Tessa said.

CHAPTER ELEVEN

Tessa couldn't remember the last time she'd been on a date. Jessica, maybe? Possibly Kory, who wasted a trip taking Tessa to a nice dimly lit restaurant when they both knew they were completely incompatible. They should have skipped dinner and that get to know you window shopping stroll, and gotten right down to business.

Sex. That's all they had had in common with each other. Their need for sex with no strings attached.

That arrangement had lasted all of a few months until Kory began to consider babies and houses and lifelong commitments.

Umm. No.

Sure, Kory was good between the sheets. But she wasn't that damn good. She wasn't toe curling, scream her name, kind of good. Truth was, no one she had met seemed worthy of making her consider the next step. Of making the U-haul leap. Of thinking beyond that box.

So they had parted ways. Kory a little scorned. Tessa unconcerned that Kory was a little scorned. And the next time their paths had crossed, when they spent five minutes too long doing the customary "How have you been? Great, and you?" Tessa knew she had made the right decision to walk away. She wasn't ready for a relationship.

Not then. Not now.

But she had to admit, Marci picking her up at the front door, opening the car door like a true gentleman, was kind of nice. Actually, it was downright sexy, and for the first time in her whole life, she'd found herself giddy with excitement.

Of course, these circumstances weren't normal. Nor were the surroundings. This place might be normal for Marci, but it surely wasn't for Tessa. She was in her dream state, fighting for her dream job. Everything was out of the norm for her.

There was romance in the air with the white ground and snow-capped branches. The fireplaces and cracking logs. The clean, crisp air and blue skies beyond the pines.

This place was a couple's dream.

But other than wanting to live in a place just like this, in a house identical to the lodge her clients got to enjoy, this wasn't Tessa's dream.

She didn't long for someone to love her. She didn't long for walking hand in hand. She didn't dream of babies or puppies or even white picket fences.

She just wanted to live. She wanted to breathe in this life and enjoy every second of it. But she wanted to do it alone. Was fine with doing it alone.

Marci reached out and took her hand. "What are you thinking about over there?"

Tessa considered lying to her. Telling her she was just enjoying the view. But regardless of where this night went, regardless of how romantic it might go, there simply wasn't room in her life for Marci right now.

The sooner she said those words out loud, the smoother the rest of this night would go.

"Just enjoying this beautiful scenery. I'm jealous you get to live with this all around you," Tessa lied, her words the exact opposite of what she planned to say.

"Well, if you win this contest, this is exactly where you'll be."

The words stunned Tessa. Sure, the prize in the game was to become the resort event planner. A resort that was well known for its lavish weddings and large seasonal crowds.

But that included Marci.

This was Marci's home. Wendy was her best friend, owner of that resort.

How would that play out when they went their separate ways only to never go their separate ways?

She would see Marci on a regular basis. She could possibly be working with her. Hell, she didn't even know what Marci's role in the resort truly was.

How awkward would that be?

"Besides being our emergency liaison, what is your job at the resort?"

"Right now, I'm nothing more than a phone clerk. I make reservations for incoming vacationers."

"So you answer phone calls? Like, in an office somewhere?" Tessa wasn't sure why that made her feel better.

"Well, don't make it sound so boring." Marci squeezed her hand, and the pressure reminded Tessa of how comfortable she was holding someone's hand. Holding Marci's hand. "To be honest, hiding in an office was my idea. I haven't played well with others since I got back. Doing the work that everyone else hates seemed like a win-win for all involved."

Tessa really wanted to pull her hand back but somehow knew she would miss the heat if she did. She also didn't want to talk about Ashley again either. Then again, she did. The more Marci talked about her, the less she would want to. Or need to.

"How long have you been back?"

"Six months? Give or take."

"What was your job in Peoria? Funny that our paths never crossed."

"Actually, they almost did. We considered using your venue, believe it or not. And I worked for a travel agent. Was the closest thing I could get to the plans I walked away from."

Tessa considered that. If Marci and Ashley had used her venue to get married. She would have gotten to know Marci as well as her cheating bride. She would have planned their magical day, right down to the flowers and food. She would have gotten to meet Marci's family and friends, all the people she loved and the ones who loved her enough to attend. She would have gotten to witness her standing tall at the altar while she waited for her bride.

The image made her uneasy.

"What kind of plans did you leave behind?"

"Just a little nonsense that seemed to work in my mind but probably would have never worked in reality."

"So tell me about it."

Marci gave her a sideways glance. Tessa couldn't tell if she was shocked that she wanted to hear all about it or if she was reluctant to share the details.

"I was considering opening up a company that would cater to select clients. Rich. Celebrity rich. Like I said, it likely wouldn't have worked out."

Tessa turned in her chair and couldn't help her sights from dripping all over Marci. From the casual grip on the steering wheel, to her angled posture in the seat just to hold Tessa's hand. She was downright delicious. Would it be bad if she asked Marci to skip all the theatrics and conversation so they could get right to the getting naked part?

"Ooh. Tell me more."

Once again, Marci gave her a puzzled glance. "Nothing much to tell now. Ashley hated Colorado. And I was chasing her skirt. That dream had a head-on collision and died right on the paper where I gave Wendy the details. So long ago it seems now."

"No dream is ever dead. It's just waylaid. And your cheating ex has nothing to do with your dream. So tell me more."

Marci wasn't sure if Tessa was being serious or just being nice. Ashley had rolled her eyes and dismissed any conversation about starting a business together. The business that she would have already begun if she hadn't chased Ashley down into the devil's den.

"I wanted a crew that would cater to a client's every need. Like an elite group of professionals. Think après-ski. With a fancy price tag."

"Who exactly are the elite clients?"

"Clients who just want to have a normal vacation away from paparazzi or prying eyes. The stars, so to speak. Famous."

"Like Denzel Washington, Elvis Presley, the president kind of famous?"

Marci threw her a smile. "Not sure I could plan an event in the afterlife, but yes, celebrity famous. Definitely not people who get to leave their homes without a bodyguard. For sure not any of the clients you guys have entertained the past weeks."

"And what would the mission be? Are we talking covert operations here? Wouldn't that need security?"

"Everything they did would be private. From shutting down a ski slope to blocking the road leading up to the lodges to even segregating a portion of a restaurant so they can dine in peace. Completely private and completely organized by a crew. All they have to do is pack their clothes and board a flight. From there, that crew caters to their every whim."

"What an amazing concept. I absolutely love it." Tessa sighed. "Sounds almost exactly like what each of us are doing now. Catering to clients. Minus the celebrity part, that is."

Marci was turned on by Tessa's admiration. By her genuine interest. It felt great to have someone interested in her dreams.

"Yeah, well, that dream died an Ashley death."

"Bullshit. That dream died a Marci death. Stop blaming Ashley for your own weakness."

Marci cut her gaze on Tessa. Her brow was arched in a serious scold. "You think I was weak because I was in love?"

"Of course not. But love shouldn't make us weak. It should make us strong. It's like one-ply toilet paper versus two-ply. Two is always better than one. So that simply means you were weak because you didn't see that she wasn't your team player before she doused your flame. She didn't make you two-ply."

Marci felt the stab of her words. How identical to Wendy's they sounded. She could be a millionaire by now if she'd charged people to tell her what she didn't know.

"I'm sorry. That was harsh. But a team player would have been thrilled to see you achieve your dreams. Ashley should have bulldozed you to the finish line and been thrilled to stand beside you every step of the way."

Tessa was right. Ashley should have been on her side. Should have had her back. Should have been happy to see Marci happy.

Fact was, she wasn't. She'd been all about Ashley, and Marci had been all about Ashley. It had been a win-win for Ashley.

Still, hearing the words, the truth behind them, didn't ease the punch of how she'd wasted so many years of her life coddling Ashley's every desire.

Never again.

When Marci didn't respond, Tessa turned back around in her chair.

She'd gone too far. Marci was still tender. Not that she would take it back or not say it again exactly the same way knowing that it would hurt Marci's feelings.

Sometimes the truth hurt. Sometimes those words needed to be said out loud. She had a sneaky suspicion Marci had had this conversation several times before. Maybe she didn't need to hear it again.

"Zen," Tessa muttered.

"What is Zen?"

"Zen. The name of your company. It implies peace. Exactly what you want for your clients." Tessa tightened her grip in Marci's hand. "Now, let's talk about something else. Like where we're going."

Marci gave her an awkward smile. "You'll see."

Tessa sank into the seat to enjoy the drive, knowing Marci was beside her thinking about her past, a dream she abandoned for love, and concentrated on the winding mountain road leading up and all of the serenity around her.

Tonight, she just wanted to enjoy herself. This date. Yes, this real date. She wanted to enjoy it because very soon, Marci would be a memory. A hot memory. She was pretty sure Marci knew it too. Maybe the words didn't need to be spoken out loud.

Thirty minutes later, Marci pulled down a long driveway tunneled under large oaks and aspen trees that ended at a single-story cottage. A thin plume of smoke seeped from a chimney.

Marci parked the car and climbed out then came around to Tessa's side while Tessa took in her surroundings with awed fascination.

In the distance, she could see the mountain ridges and cliffs, all white and beautiful. Did people run out of things to do with such beauty around them? Did they get tired of seeing so much white? Did they get sick of being snowed in their homes?

Tessa didn't see how. She'd love to be trapped inside with a fireplace, food, and sex. It would be the perfect blizzard conditions.

Marci opened the door and Tessa blinked out of her trance.

She finally stepped out. "A cottage in the middle of nowhere? What? I'm not worth a movie in town with all of those sparkly streetlights? Candlelit dinner at a five-star restaurant?" she teased her and scooted around the door. "I gave up the goodies too fast, didn't I?"

"You don't strike me as the cheesy dinner and movie type of girl." Marci winked and shut the door. "As for the goodies, I might require you to put out before the date is over."

Tessa looked back to the cottage. "I'm not easy, stud. Let's see if you deserve it. Or better, earn it."

Marci took her hand and led her toward the house. Instead of going onto the porch where two wicker-back rockers sat, she veered them to a path that led around the side of the house and toward the backyard.

When they reached a bend in the path, Marci turned to Tessa.

Tessa was hoping, praying, that Marci was going to tug her against her chest. That she was going to kiss her so hard she'd feel it all the way to her toes.

"Close your eyes," Marci said.

"Is this a trust me and I promise not to let you walk off a cliff, kind of challenge?"

"No, this is a close your eyes so you don't ruin my surprise, kind of demand."

"I don't do demands. Haven't you met me yet?"

Marci bent down, scooped Tessa up by her ass, and slung her over her shoulder.

Tessa let out a squeal while her insides clamped down tight. She'd never been manhandled before and she damn sure liked it.

Marci spun around and continued walking as if Tessa weighed nothing. It was sexy how strong she was. More sexy that she had shut off Tessa's teasing argument so quickly.

For sure, she would be putting out tonight.

Marci finally stopped and set Tessa on her feet, and before Tessa could pretend to argue, Marci stepped into her and crushed their lips together.

Tessa moaned while her body hummed with electric energy. She was going to miss this. These kisses. Those hands. All that magical bliss from Marci's knees.

All of it. Tessa knew she was going to miss something, someone, for the first time in her life.

Marci finally pulled away. "Welcome to our date." She stepped to the side and waved her hand toward the backyard.

A double thick king-size air mattress covered in blankets was positioned directly beneath a large pergola. Sheer fabric was draped on all sides, almost hiding the inside. Tall heaters sat at every corner, and a fire pit was off to one side.

Tessa was shocked. It was perfect. All of it. No one had ever gone to so much trouble for a date. Movies. Dinners. Walks through the park. Sometimes none of the above, just directly to the sex.

Touched, she looked from the little slice of paradise, feeling an emotion that was foreign to her, back to Marci. A look of pure admiration washed over her face. How in the world was she going to tell Marci that their time was limited? Did she already know? Could she feel it? Like Tessa felt it?

Tessa suddenly regretted saying yes to this date tonight. Every minute she spent with Marci was pushing off the inevitable. Every sweet thing that Marci did, Tessa was taking another step back from putting an end to their glorious times.

Soon. She had to say something soon.

"You did this for me?" She glanced back to the setup, taking in the wine bottles in a bucket of ice, wine glasses cushioned by a red towel in a wicker basket. It was too romantic. For couples in love. Couples searching for love. Not for Tessa, who was doing anything but searching for a commitment.

Marci took her hand and led her to the mattress.

Tessa crawled into the center while Marci poured glasses of wine and handed her one. She held out her glass for a toast.

"To a great friend, to the benefits of that great friend, to winning this contest, and to getting on with my new life. And for you getting back to yours," Tessa blurted, regretting how eager and rushed her words sounded.

Marci watched her for several seconds before she clinked her glass against Tessa's. "Okay. To that."

She curled up on the mattress and leaned back against the pillows. "So tell me more about your family. Are your parents alive?"

"Yes. They both live in Peoria. My dad married Monty's mom right after she was born and my mom works in a bank and still plans events in her spare time."

"Wait. Does that mean…"

"That my dad cheated on my mom? Yes. Monty is living proof that my dad wasn't faithful."

"Wow. I'm sorry. That must have sucked."

"Don't be. Shit happens for a reason."

Marci looked stunned for a minute, as if she couldn't believe Tessa was taking such a horrible experience so lightly, then she looked back to her wine glass.

"Don't get me wrong. Our lives were rocked for a while. Michelle hated him. She wouldn't even speak to him. And even now, she barely has anything to do with Monty, as if a baby could be to blame."

"What about your mom? How did she take it?"

"She was sad for a while. We could tell. But she kept right on moving. She never let us see her fall apart. And when Monty got a little older, she even let me babysit her overnight at home."

"Your mom sounds like a tough one. I see where you get all your sweet charm." Marci scrunched her nose.

"Damn right. She showed me how to get cut off at the knees and still finish the race."

"And your sex-addicted little sister?"

Tessa sighed. "Monty. The apple of her mother's eye, the thorn in my father's side, and a person who might be genuinely hated by Michelle." She added a snicker. "I hate her habits. So, so bad I hate her habits. But I adore her. She's seriously my best friend. I can't wait for you to meet her."

Confused by her confession, Tessa tilted the glass to her lips.

She wasn't sure why she'd said those last words. Sucked more that she really meant them. There wasn't anything wrong with wanting to introduce Marci to her sister. Or was there? It wasn't like she was bringing home a girl to meet her mother. Right?

Marci took a sip of wine then propped her head in her hand. She tagged Tessa in those chocolate eyes, and suddenly, Tessa didn't want to talk about Ashley, careers, Monty, the contest, the new life that awaited her, or even that Tessa was going to blister her feelings very soon.

She leaned over and pressed her lips against Marci's. Mainly to ease her own tension of what was to come.

But not tonight.

Tonight she just wanted to feel free.

That tingling sensation swept along her body as Marci deepened the kiss.

She needed to be closer. Wanted to feel Marci's heat and the protection she felt when she was in those arms.

With a hungry growl, Tessa straddled her and took her wine glass. She set the glasses on the ground haphazardly then pushed their lips together again.

This time, sex was different. This time, they undressed each other with detailed precision, kissing skin as it was bared, memorizing and exploring until they both cried out their release.

Tessa was in trouble.

Without a shadow of a doubt, she knew she was in trouble.

Soon. She had to end this. So very soon.

Chapter Twelve

That bitch missed her flight!" Tessa growled and tossed the phone on the couch. "I can't believe it!"

"From what you've told me about your sister, I can't believe that *you* can't believe that," Seth said from the chair beside her. He reached out and squeezed her arm. "Stop panicking. You should be freaking out right now! We just made it into the finale!" He squealed out his last word, and Tessa felt that giddy emotion quicken in her stomach.

Yes! They'd done that. They'd won top points once again. Her team was one of only two teams still standing.

Holy hell but she was inches away from having her life spin out from under her feet. Only one more client. Only one more week of planning. Only one more to conquer. Just one more.

And then she could be swept into a frenzy of weddings. Would be. She was going to win this thing or leave a trail of blood and tears all the way back to Arizona or lock herself in one of the resort bathrooms and refuse to leave the premises. Either way, she wouldn't go down quietly.

That close. Oh my God. She was that close to being *the* shit in the wedding industry, in *the* resort that dominated the most prestigious wedding locations.

"I'm sorry." Tessa made what she hoped was a genuine pouty face when the need to grind her teeth in irritation was so strong.

Monty was going to try her nerves, and this was the one time she didn't need any added stress.

"But she knows how important tonight is and I'm so, so sick of her self-centered ass," Tessa growled.

She actually didn't know just how sick she was of Monty's self-absorbed ways until this exact moment. Was it too much to ask that she put her sluts aside for a single fucking week? Was it too much to ask to have her undivided attention for just a fraction of a minute? Just one weekend. That's all she needed. That was all of Monty's time she'd asked for.

Yes. Obviously, trying to depend on Monty was too much to ask. Michelle had warned her this would happen when Tessa announced that Monty was coming for moral support during the finale. An offer Michelle had refused as soon as she heard that Monty had accepted.

She couldn't even depend on Monty for the most important challenge in her life. And Tessa was damn tired of always being the mothering adult and trying to keep her in line. Damn tired of it.

"Why don't we go spend the day up at the lodge? We can get ahead of ourselves for next week," Seth said.

Tessa faked a smile. This awesome guy had opted out of going into town today with the rest of the overly excited crew members. Instead, he decided to stay behind to hang out with Tessa. To help her get the lodge ready and wait for Monty. The Monty who had missed her flight. The Monty who promised, no matter what, she would be on time to spend the day with Tessa, to help her stay calm and celebrate tonight with her.

And now Seth was stuck with Tessa who was in a foul mood and ready to call the Peoria radio station and have them make a public announcement that her sister had cooties.

Poor Seth. He was such a sweetheart. All of them were, actually. She'd been extremely blessed to have gained a crew that was on board no matter what crazy decision Tessa had made.

No matter what ridiculous thing she changed. No matter how many times she repeated that process. They'd never questioned her antics and had seemed happy and eager to go with the flow, soaking up everything as a learning experience, and jumping to pull their own weight.

She could only hope, win or lose, that she'd taught them something about giving everything they had to reach the next goal in life. To never give up. To never give in.

For most of them, those who weren't content in their current positions, she prayed she'd showed them that she wasn't afraid to not only think outside the box, but to create and build a larger, better, fancier box around that one. It would make her heart happy to know she'd given them the courage to keep pushing ahead until they reached their personal goals.

She knew bigger and better opportunities awaited them. Their team had been noticed. Their names were now out there. Each of them. Who they were, what they did, and where they came from. It was just a matter of time before they each took their leaps, and nothing made her happier than to think she'd help make a difference in the lives.

"I think you should stop worrying about the lodge and take your ass down this mountain to hang out with the rest of our crew." Tessa arched a brow at him. "I'm just gonna be a Debbie Downer until Monty shows her face. If she does. And when—if—she does, you might not want to be a witness to the crimes I have in mind."

"She will make it. Just wait and see. And hanging with a Debbie Downer is way better than Slut Sally, Hoe Hunter, or Do Them All Danny." Seth cocked his head and pursed his lips. "Do you know how hard it is to stop three drunk sex addicts from diving headfirst into an STD? It's not pretty."

"Danny? Quiet, OCD, Danny?"

"Girl, please. He'd get a knothole pregnant if there wasn't someone sane, meaning me, and not drunk, also me, around to stop him." Seth lifted his arm above his head and pointed at himself in a perfect Blake Shelton move. "Me. Sane one. Only sober one during every celebration thanks to his need to reproduce with things dead or alive."

Tessa giggled. "I'll never be able to look at him the same again. Sweet Danny, a sex fiend. Hilarious."

"Sally is far worse, as if that doesn't come as a surprise." He wagged his finger. "I can't believe you didn't know she screwed Terry from Cynthia's team. When their team got sent home, she started sleeping with Carl from Donald's team. Who knows who she'll turn to now that his team is out."

"No. No way. Terry was married and Carl was gay. Wasn't he?"

Seth gave a firm nod. "Apparently, Sally has that magic touch." He pressed his index finger against his lips.

The phone rang and Tessa snatched it off the cushion and glanced at the screen before accepting the call. "You better be boarding that flight or so help me God I will announce to every female, in every club, in every city and town, in the whole state of Arizona that you have serious venereal diseases. Incurable, blistery, warty, smelly, gooey diseases."

"Do you kiss our daddy with that mouth?" Monty asked.

Commotion and stomping rang through the phone. Incoherent announcements blared through a speaker system.

"I'm not kidding, Monty! I'm pissed and excited and worried and you're not here!"

"Calm down, Tess. I'm boarding the plane as we speak. I swear."

"Then why the fuck are you running?" Tessa shoved off the couch, the anger overtaking her emotions. "I can hear you stomping, dumbass!"

Was it horrible that she wanted her sister here? Needed her here for the last charge of this race. She needed Monty's no-nonsense attitude. The one that always calmed Tessa when she was upset or over-emotional. She needed Monty to calm her fears and anxiety.

Dammit. Why couldn't Monty just do one simple thing right? Why did she have to let her down this time, of all times?

"Breathe, Tess. Just breathe. I'll be there in three hours."

Monty disconnected the call and Tessa fell back on the couch with a growl.

"I can totally see her running through the airport, half naked, one shoe on, hair completely amok, lipstick stains on her neck, and bitches will still stop her just to get her number. And she'll flirt long and hard before she finally gives out those digits because that's how my little fuck everyone sister performs. And then she'll miss her fucking flight while I sit here and brew and then give me some cockamamie excuse about how it wasn't her fault."

"No, ma'am. We're not doing this, this pouting thing another second. You're not allowed to sit here and stew when we're this close to being crowned winners." Seth pushed out of the chair. "So get your ass up from there and let's go put that anger to good use because in case you haven't noticed, I kind of like crowns." He struck a queen-worthy pose, then tugged her off the couch.

Four hours and a cleanly stocked lodge later, Tessa stepped onto the porch of their cabin to find Monty perched on the swing, arm dangling over the back, foot propped up on the arm, eating a banana. With, apparently, not a damn care in the world.

The anger she'd attempted to erase while she cleaned her favorite place, that amazing lodge with its spacious rooms and incredible views, drained as soon as Monty flashed her that perfect smile and rose from the swing.

Tessa couldn't help herself. Relief flooded. She raced across the porch and flung her arms around Monty's neck.

Her worries and fears melted away as Monty lifted her off her feet in a bear hug and spun her around. Monty's hugs always had a way of taking away the anxiety.

"There, there, big sister. I'm here to make it all better."

And she would. She had that special something that made Tessa forget what she was upset about. Had that smooth demeanor that made her not care about the bad anymore. Monty was the one who let her know everything was going to be okay, even if it wasn't.

Monty sat her back on her feet and Tessa slapped her arm. "Ouch. What the…"

Tessa playfully smacked her again. "You're an asshole, Monty! Couldn't you, for one single fucking night, keep your dick in your pants?"

Monty cupped her crotch with one hand. "What does my dick have to do with anything?"

"You missed your flight, asswipe. The other group leader has his entire family on deck." Tessa poked her finger into Monty's chest, trying her best to keep the smile from forming. "Yet my very own sister is the slack ass."

Seth stepped around Tessa and shoved his hand out. "I'm Seth. One of her crew members. Her favorite crew member, I feel obliged to include."

Monty tossed the last bite of banana over the railing and hugged him instead. "Poor, poor Seth. I've heard tons of great things about you. And I've sent up several prayers for your survival while working for this one." She released him and patted his arm. "I see my pleas worked. You're welcome."

"I'm gonna keep my response to myself as I'm sure you understand." He gave a bright smile and tossed a cautious glance at Tessa. "But I've heard tons about you as well. Tessa absolutely hates to adore you." He playfully backed out of swinging range. "Don't smack me! I'm not as solid as your sister."

Tessa smirked. "Monty is the only one I abuse. She always deserves it."

Monty snaked her arm around Tessa's neck and drew her close. "You love me and you know it. So let's go inside before we freeze our lady parts off."

"And so you can get a damn shower. We have to be down at the resort in less than two hours for interviews."

"My sister. A celebrity." She gave Tessa another squeeze. "I can't wait to photobomb your moment. And then meet your hot new girlfriend."

Seth opened the front door and they all moved inside.

"She is not my girlfriend," Tessa said.

Monty casually looked toward Seth as if looking for confirmation.

Seth held up his hands defensively. "I'm out of this argument." He took several steps away and adamantly nodded his head at Monty.

"I saw that!" Tessa said.

Seth scooted around the back of the couch with a wicked smile, then disappeared into his room.

"So when do I get to meet this not your hot new girlfriend?" Monty shucked out of her coat and hung it by the door.

"My friend with benefits, who has kept me from losing my mind through this whole ordeal, will be at the party along with my boss, Wendy."

"Ah. The boss. I like badass female bosses. I want to meet the boss."

Tessa cocked her hands on her hips. "I suggest you draw that thought right back into the deepest part of your dirty mind. If you so much as wink at her, I will shove you off this mountain." She gave her best "try me" glare.

"Oh, sweet, sweet Tess. Have a little more faith in your perfect little sister. A few minutes alone with her, working a little tongue action, and that new job will be all yours."

"Monty!"

Monty laughed and hugged Tessa. "I'm kidding! I'm kidding. Where has your sense of humor gone?"

"Go get in the damn shower before I show you where it went." She pushed away from Monty and pointed toward her bedroom door. "Step on it."

Monty grabbed the handle of her suitcase and started for the bedroom. "I'm your biggest fan, you know? And I'm so proud of you."

Tessa was too choked up to respond. God, she loved her butthead, self-centered little sister.

All fucked up parts of her included.

❖

Marci couldn't stop watching the doorway. Even with the crowd, her focus remained on that door. On every face walking through it.

A few photographers from the surrounding radio and news stations roamed the room, stopping periodically to snap a photo of the two remaining crews, ask a few questions, and then jot notes down in their notebooks.

Even with all of the commotion, the loud chatter, and periodic interruption, her attention remained on that opening, knowing any second Tessa was going to walk through it. No doubt with her beloved little sister, Monty, who appeared to be the mature black sheep of the family. If there was such a thing.

Marci was nervous. Something she rarely ever was. Though she shouldn't be. Tessa wasn't her girlfriend. Or even a great friend. It wasn't like she was meeting Tessa's parents. But for some reason, she knew Monty's approval meant everything to Tessa.

That made this introduction far more important than a parent meet and greet.

Again, it shouldn't matter. She and Tessa would be going their separate ways very soon. Marci could feel it. Tessa might not have said those words out loud, but the words were there hiding beneath the surface nonetheless.

Soon, she was going to hear them and she wasn't sure how she felt about it. She liked Tessa. That was impossible considering the hell she'd been through this past year. That was impossible because she'd built the damn brick wall to avoid such things from happening. She'd made it sturdy and impossible to penetrate.

Or so she thought.

But the fact remained the same. She liked Tessa. Too much. And she dreaded the day that Tessa finally gathered her courage and told her their time had come to a close.

"You haven't cussed anyone out yet. I'm impressed." Wendy handed her a Corona.

"Yet. The night is still young." Marci's gaze swung toward the door again.

"She's outside with the reporters doing interviews."

"Who?"

"Oh please." Wendy rolled her eyes. "Don't even pretend you haven't been eyeballing that damn door for the past thirty minutes." She lifted her wrist to inspect bare skin. "Oh, wait. Appears I lost track of time. For the past hour."

Marci considered arguing with her, then thought better. That was exactly what she'd been doing. Waiting with bated breath.

"Just anxious to meet this sister of hers. She's gone on and on about her."

"Uh-huh." Wendy turned up her bottle and eyed Marci. "I'm sure that's the only reason."

Marci ignored her insinuation and forced her attention away from the door. One more week and this contest would come to a close. No more stolen moments with Tessa. No more secret adventures under the waterfalls. No more watching her from afar as she explored the great outdoors. No more.

Exactly the way it should be. Marci could go back to where she left off weeks ago. Back to her office with nothing more than the voices on the other end of the line to bother her. Hiding from the world and taking home the women whose names she had no desire to know.

Damn, she couldn't wait.

Tessa stepped inside the conference room and spotted Marci immediately. Across the room with Wendy. Looking tall and sexy.

Her heart fluttered with the thought. She hated that flutter. More than anything, she hated that fucking flutter. It meant she'd crossed a line. It meant she'd played too long. Stayed too long. Waited too long.

Waited too long for herself or for Marci, she wasn't sure. Dammit. She'd simply waited too long.

Marci wasn't the one she'd been looking for. She was broken and still hadn't put herself back together. She was scorned and untrusting. She was everything Tessa didn't want in her life.

Yet she couldn't still her quickening heart and made a promise to have that long overdue talk with Marci very, very soon.

Monty took two wine glasses off the table and joined Tessa. She held one out. "Here. Take a drink. Then another. You're wound too tight. This is supposed to be a celebration. Act like it."

Tessa took the drink and looked up at Monty. "One more week. My new life could begin in a single week."

Monty tapped their glasses together. "Oh you will, awesome sister. You most certainly will." She glanced around the room. "Now, show her to me."

Tessa turned back to Marci, excited to finally introduce Monty to the person she'd talked so much about, to put a face to all the stories she'd told Monty during their phone conversations over the past few weeks.

"There." She nodded toward Marci.

Marci's gaze turned on her, and Tessa's gut tightened as those sexy brown eyes locked on her.

Tessa smiled and waved, knowing it was middle school stupidity. Dammit, she wasn't crushing out. But damn if she wasn't.

Trouble. She was in so much trouble.

Marci raised her hand, and then the smile melted off her face and a mask of rage transformed her expression.

"Oh shit," Monty whispered.

Tessa turned to look at her. She wore an expression Tessa had never seen on her tough and always unfazed little sister.

Paralyzed fear. Monty looked terrified.

"What is it?" Tessa grabbed her hand.

Monty never averted her sights from across the room. "Tess, I'm so sorry. This is going to be disastrous."

Tessa turned back to Marci.

Those hate-filled eyes bored into her.

Tessa had a sinking feeling in the pit of her stomach as Marci bent down to say something to Wendy, who promptly turned toward Tessa and Monty.

What the hell was going on? And why did she feel like a weight had just been dropped on her?

"For your sake, I have to get out of here." Monty slammed her glass down and escaped back through the door.

Tessa stood frozen, unsure what direction to turn. Run after Monty? Stay for her personal celebration? Walk away from Marci's angry expression?

What the fuck was going on, and why was something deep down telling her she already knew?

But no matter what, she would always follow her sister. Always.

Tessa set her glass down and ran after Monty.

CHAPTER THIRTEEN

"Marci, you need to calm down," Wendy pleaded. "This isn't the time or the place for drama."

"How could she bring that, that slut here?" Marci could feel the irrational words ringing back on her ears but couldn't stop herself from saying them out loud.

Wendy stepped in front of her, trying to pull her focus away from the doorway through which Tessa and her piece of shit sister had just vanished. It was all she could do not to run after her, to scream, to fucking kick something and make an absolute ass of herself.

"That woman is her sister." Wendy squeezed her arm. "Please calm down. I'm positive there's a reasonable explanation."

Marci could hear the logic in Wendy's words, but she'd never been so enraged. Not even the day she opened the bedroom door to witness her life going up in flames. With that woman, Monty, Tessa's beloved little sister, staring back at her.

Right now, she was too far gone to calm down, to even talk herself out of the ugly thoughts swarming in her mind.

"I fucking told you, Wendy." Marci pulled out of Wendy's grasp and squeezed her palm into a fist then loosened the pressure, wanting to follow Tessa, not wanting to follow either of them, knowing it would be a huge mistake to go through that door, but not sure she had a choice. "I told you she was up to no good!"

"Marci, listen to what you're saying. Tessa looked genuinely confused. I don't think she has a clue what is happening right now."

"Bullshit," Marci spat. "She knew."

"Look, you need to calm down and think about what you're saying. I can't talk to you when you're like this." Wendy threw up her hand. "Just give everyone a minute to calm down and then you—"

"Minute's up." Marci dropped the beer bottle in the trash and charged across the room.

"Marci! Stop!" Wendy yelled.

But Marci couldn't stop. Not this time.

She felt stupid, betrayed, backstabbed as she moved around people and shot out of the conference room.

Tessa spotted Monty far down the sidewalk, pacing in front of a line of parked cars. Her shoulders were slumped. Her hands shoved in her front pockets.

The tightening in Tessa's stomach only gripped harder as she got closer. Her sister never showed defeat. Nor did she ever look defeated. Never. And right now, she looked like the whole world rested solely on her shoulders.

Monty looked up and Tessa could read complete shock in those eyes.

It was another expression she'd never seen.

Monty never felt bad. She never regretted anything. Said she never did anything to have to regret.

But right now, Tessa was seeing regret eating her sister alive, and it made her nauseous.

Under any other circumstances, she might be grateful to see life in those eyes. Something other than her uncaring demeanor.

But not here. Not with a celebration, her celebration, taking place inside that building. Not when she had a horrible, gut-wrenching suspicion that she knew exactly what had prodded Monty into this abnormal behavior.

No. This wasn't a suspicion knotting her stomach. She knew better.

Monty was the one. She was the one Marci had caught in bed with her wife. Naked. Watching Marci as if waiting for her to charge. Marci had said that. That the woman didn't even bother covering herself. Simply stared back at her and never attempted to move.

That was exactly what Monty would have done. She'd been caught, so why try to run? Why try to hide? Besides, it wasn't Monty who had anything to run from. She wasn't the married woman. She wasn't the one who was supposed to be faithful.

Tessa came to a stop beside her and took a deep breath. "It was you, wasn't it?"

Monty glanced over at her but immediately looked down at her feet. "You should go back inside, Tess. I'm ruining your party."

"Say it, Monty." Tessa circled around her, forcing Monty to look at her. "You will goddamn say it out loud!"

"Tess. I said I was sorry." Monty's shoulders rose. "I don't know what else I can say. What do you want from me?"

"Of all the women in the whole town and you picked that one." Tessa shook her head. "What the fuck, Monty?"

"How could I have known?"

Anger bubbled hard and fast as she heard the "oh, woe is me" in Monty's words. "That's the problem. You don't care to know. You never care. With wedding bands or with photos of kids tucked in their cell phones, you just don't give a shit. And now your karma will rain down on me."

Monty turned around and grabbed Tessa's hands. "Tell me what you want me to do, Tess, and I'll do it. If you want me to leave, I'll leave. If you want me to go beg her forgiveness, I'll do that. Please just tell me. I've never felt more worthless in my life than I do right now." Her eyes welled with tears, and it was all Tessa could manage not to hug her tight and tell her everything was going to be okay. "You know I would never do anything to hurt you. You know that."

Tessa couldn't hug Monty. She couldn't tell her everything was going to be okay. Because right now, she wasn't sure anything was going to be okay. Wasn't sure it was ever going to be okay again. She didn't have a magic solution, but one thing she did know, Monty was being genuine. She would never deliberately hurt Tessa. That fact she would go to her grave knowing.

"Can you do me a favor?" Tessa mumbled.

"Anything." Monty's shoulders lifted and her posture heightened.

"Next time you need attention, just fucking photobomb my ass."

Monty stared for several seconds before she finally cracked a smile.

Tessa wasn't sure why she felt the need to put that smile on Monty's face, but it sure beat the alternative. That sad expression was one she never wanted to see again. Even if Monty had done something horribly wrong.

"How dare you bring that piece of shit here!" Marci bellowed.

Tessa spun around to find Marci marching down the sidewalk, Wendy running behind her.

This was embarrassing. Too dramatic. This was her minute. Dammit. Her time. Her future and possibly her new world.

And Monty's inability to keep her hands to herself was going to make it all crumble down around her.

"Marci! Stop it right now!" Wendy yelled through clenched teeth as she grabbed for Marci, clearly shaken by the drama unfolding without her control.

Tessa hated that more than anything. That her boss was involved in any of this. But at least they had one thing in common. Both of the people they loved the most in the world couldn't act right.

"I'm sorry, Tess. I truly am," Monty mumbled beside her.

"I know. But you're still on my shit list."

Tessa focused on Marci, her angry posture as she pounded down the sidewalk, her heart knowing Marci wouldn't do anything stupid. If she was going to stoop that low, she would have done it the day she caught Monty fucking her wife.

No. Tessa wasn't afraid of that. But she needed Marci to know where her loyalty lay.

She did the only thing she knew how to do. The only thing she would ever know how to do. The only thing a good sister should ever do.

She stepped in front of Monty and lifted her chin. Right or wrong, Monty was her sister, and no matter how disgusted Tessa was with her actions, she'd never let anyone threaten or hurt her.

Not even Marci. Especially not Marci.

Marci came to a breathless stop a few feet from Tessa, her eyes drilling into Tessa's. "What kind of sick game have you been playing?"

"Oh, God. That again?" Tessa controlled the need to roll her eyes.

Maric's gaze darted to Monty then stabbed back on Tessa. "You knew all along, didn't you? Admit it!"

The anger in Marci's eyes made Tessa sad for some reason. Ashley had done a number on her confidence. She'd pushed Marci into this sheltered, non-trusting space, and it was ugly coming out of her.

"Knew what, Marci? Tell me."

"That she fucked my wife! That's what!" Marci took a step closer, looking enraged.

"Not until two minutes ago. It's not like I keep up with the notches on my sister's bedpost." Tessa planted her hands on her hips, damned if Marci was going to point fingers all over again. "Do you even hear how incredibly ridiculous you sound right now?"

"I'm the one you have an issue with. Not her. Let Tess go enjoy her night then you can yell and scream at me all you want," Monty quietly said.

Marci's jaw clenched. "Shut up, you home wrecking twerp. No one is talking to you."

"Marci. Please go back inside. This isn't the time," Wendy pleaded and tugged Marci's arm.

Marci pulled her arm free. "When was the time, Tessa? Tell me? When were you going to tell me that it was your sister who fucked up my whole world?"

Tessa angled her head and studied that angry expression. Even with her eyes wide, her mouth set and grim, she was so handsome. But she was damaged. So damaged.

"It wasn't my sister who fucked you over, Marci. That person was Ashley. Your wife. Your wife did this to you. Not Monty. And the sooner you get that through your thick skull, the faster you can move on with life."

Marci felt the sting of her words. The calm way in which she'd said them. The identical words Wendy had been preaching for months now. But what she saw was Tessa standing in front of a lowlife, guarding her, protecting the very person who was the cause of her entire world shattering.

She was protecting her sister. Siding with her.

Marci stepped forward again, knowing she shouldn't. She was too angry. Too hurt. "Go to hell, Tessa."

Wendy lightly tugged her arm again as Monty pulled Tessa back and stepped in front her.

She leveled daring eyes on Marci. "I'll say it one more time. Your problem lies with me. Not her. If you want to talk, we'll talk. If you want to take it out in the parking lot, we can do that too. But if you take one more step toward my sister, this night is going to end in disaster, and from all the great things Tess had told me about you, it doesn't sound like you want that ending." She lifted her chin. "But I need you to know that choice is completely yours."

Marci tightened her hands into fists, not liking the challenge in those eyes. Not sure she could walk away from the dare. From the *choice*.

Wendy tightened her grip in warning. "Marci. Right now. Get your ass walking right this second."

Marci moved her focus to Tessa. To those sad eyes. To those beautiful, sad eyes. She hated herself for letting Tessa into her world. Hated that she'd let her guard down.

She looked back to Monty, the very sister Tessa had told her so much about, the very one she admired for her accomplishments, for her maturity, she'd said, but who hated one little thing about her. That very little thing had ripped her marriage apart. That very thing was why Marci was far away from the place she'd made home. Why she was still hurt and angry at the whole damn world.

And Tessa was standing only feet away from her, protecting and siding with that very piece of shit.

"Stay the fuck away from me." Marci narrowed her gaze on Monty. "Both of you." She pulled away from Wendy and charged down the sidewalk.

Tessa watched her retreating steps, wanting to go after her, to beg her to see how wrong she was, that Monty wasn't the bad guy here, but she knew it would be a useless attempt tonight.

Marci was too angry. Too hurt. And Tessa couldn't truly blame her. Deep down, she was blaming Monty as well. Of course, she knew it wasn't Monty's fault that Ashley had cheated on her, but it sure felt that way at this moment when a party was waiting for her inside, where her crew was probably wondering what in the world was going on.

Wendy turned a frown on Tessa. "I'm sorry, Tessa. I tried to stop her."

"No. I'm the one who is sorry. This is all too much." Tessa shook her head. "Talk about dumb luck."

Monty entwined their fingers and gave a squeeze. "Tell me what I can do?"

"You can stop asking me what you can do. You might not want the answer." Tessa tried to add a notch of teasing to her words although she wasn't completely against rolling Monty off this mountain.

That would sure solve one problem.

Dammit. Of all the women, it had to be Ashley. What kind of shit luck was that?

"I know it's all crazy right now, but tomorrow is a new day. Give Marci some alone time with her thoughts and I'm positive she'll see how ridiculous she is." Wendy extended her hand to Monty. "I'm Wendy, by the way. Best friend to that hothead. And under normal circumstances, I'd hug the living shit out of you. I hated Ashley with every ounce of my body."

Monty lightly took her hand and looked down the length of Wendy. "You can still hug me. I won't mind a bit." She gave that sweet smile.

"I will drop-kick you off a cliff," Tessa growled.

Monty laughed and let go of Wendy's hand. "I'm kidding, big sister. Just trying to bring some light to the dark moment."

"It will be good and dark at the bottom of this mountain." Tessa cocked a brow. "Don't try me right now."

Wendy snickered. "You guys are cute, and as much as I'd like to stay and help make the dark moment bright, I need to go check on Marci." She reached out and patted Tessa's hand. "And I know everything looks bleak right now, but Marci is a great person and this isn't her normal behavior. Seeing your sister was just too much. Everything will be okay. I promise."

Tessa gave a tight nod, still considering going inside to make an attempt to talk to Marci. Her inner voice objected too loud, and right now she had to listen to anything that sounded sane.

"Thanks, Wendy. And I'm so sorry about this," Tessa added.

"I wish I could say the same. But I can't." Wendy gave Monty a flirtatious wink. "It was great meeting you, Monty. I hope to see you around during the week."

Monty nodded. "That's a must."

Tessa watched Wendy make her way down the sidewalk, her words ringing back on her ears, and she knew what she had to do.

"Take me home, Monty."

"You mean the cabin?"

"No. Home. Home." Tessa turned and started for the Jeep. "I quit."

Chapter Fourteen

Tessa leaned against the railing, her sights trained on Marci's cabin. Her heart ached. Why, she didn't know. She hadn't done anything wrong. Yet she still felt like everything was her fault.

She just wanted Marci to listen to her. To hear her. To see how crazy this whole thing was. But most of all, she wanted to look Marci in the eye with every word, to make sure she got it.

Four times this morning alone, she'd gone to Marci's cabin to knock on the door, the fourth was full on banging, yelling for her to open the fucking door and to stop being such an immature toddler, hoping that her words would piss Marci off enough to jerk the door open.

It hadn't.

She had no idea what she would have said if she'd been faced with Marci's enraged stare again, but she knew she had to say something. Had to get it off her chest once and for all.

This was all insane. Completely and ridiculously insane. What were the odds that Monty, her very own sister, was the one who crushed Marci's world? Yet here she was, living the reality.

And if not for Monty and Seth talking her off the ledge last night, she would have packed her bags and left this contest. She was still prepared to. Ready to get the hell off this mountain, away from Marci, out of her life forever, because that's what she thought was best.

Not for herself. But for Marci.

And here she stood in the freezing cold, watching Marci's cabin for any sign of movement. Praying she would change her mind and open the door, motion her over, and have makeup sex right after she told her off for being so over-the-top.

But the longer she stood on the porch, the more she realized that wasn't going to happen. Marci wasn't going to invite her in. She wasn't going to sit down and talk this out.

That made her even madder. And clueless. Lost. Why did she feel so lost? Why was she still so mad? And sad. And confused.

One minute she was blaming Marci for being out of her mind. The next, she blamed Monty for being such a slut. The next, she felt that fighting spirit she'd inherited from her mother take back control, and she wanted to tell them both to go fuck themselves.

This was truly the most twisted scenario she'd ever found herself in. Utterly and completely twisted.

The door opened behind her, and Tessa looked down into her mug of coffee that was probably as cold as the ice crystal dripping off the trees for as long as she'd been staring across the distance to Marci's house.

Monty joined her against the railing.

"Will it help for me to say I'm sorry again?"

"No."

"Then stop."

"Stop what?" Tessa took a sip of her coffee and as suspected, it was freezing cold.

"That face." Monty propped her foot against the rail. "Don't do that face."

"I don't have a face." Tessa poured the coffee over the porch and set the mug down.

"Yes, you do. It's a defeated face. It's a white towel waving kind of face. We Daltons don't do defeated faces."

Tessa glanced toward Marci's cabin. Was she there? Had she been ignoring Tessa all morning, watching her trek through the snow, through the trees, all the way to her cabin, watching Tessa through the curtain like a coward?

"I'm fine."

"No, you're not. You're mad. She's mad. And I'm the root of it all."

"You're not the root, Monty. And the more you say that, the more pissed I get at you. So stop."

"Fine. I'll shut up. But please don't throw in the towel, Tess. You've bossed your way through this whole contest. Don't you dare bow out now. I'd never be able to forgive myself."

It sucked that Monty was right about one thing. The Dalton girls weren't allowed to show defeat. It was a sign of weakness. And they didn't do weak. However, Tessa had always assumed she and Michelle had gotten that independence from their mother. After all, it was their mother who had held all the pieces together while their father got to start a brand new life, brand new wife, brand new house, and a brand new baby that turned out to be the most glorious, hellacious thorn in Tessa's side. God, how she loved that little brat. The very one blaming herself right now.

Yet Monty possessed that strong will also. Possibly far stronger than she or Michelle. So had they inherited that watch me win gene from their father? Unlikely. As awesome as he was, as much as she loved him, he was weak. He couldn't say no. Hadn't said no. His weakness had cost him dearly. Was still costing him. Tessa wasn't sure his bond with Michelle would ever be repaired. Likely, after all of these years, it never would be.

Yet their mother had never blamed Monty's mother. Not once. Even when her world was spinning out of control, she hadn't blamed the wrong person. Her finger had always stayed pointed at their father. Exactly where it deserved to be pointed.

Maybe Tessa should send her mother to have a word of prayer with Marci. Surely she could set her twisted mind straight.

Suddenly, her sorrow turned into a bit of anger.

Why was she the one waiting for Marci to show herself across the woods? Why was she the one banging on her door all morning? She hadn't done anything wrong. Neither had Monty. Marci was her own worst enemy, and Tessa needed to lift her chin and drive right back into the game. She should have never taken her eyes off the prize in the first place. Her intrigue over Marci had made her do that. She'd succumbed to lust and it was biting her in the ass right now.

Marci would never see how wrong she was. She didn't want to. She needed someone to blame. Needed to blame the wrong person. And as much as Tessa could understand why, she couldn't keep dwelling on an outcome that wasn't going to change. An outcome she couldn't change.

Monty would always be her sister. A sister she loved no matter what.

Meanwhile, more importantly, the new client's video was waiting for her to view. A contest was waiting for her to win.

A new life was just around the corner.

It was all hers for the taking.

Fuck Marci and her brick wall.

Fuck her.

Tessa snagged her mug off the banister and spun toward the door. "Let's get to work."

"Now you're talking!"

Marci listened to the secretary take yet another phone call while she sat in the lobby waiting for her lawyer to prepare the paperwork for both the closing on the house as well as her divorce papers. Two birds. One stone.

She was more ready than she thought to get this final step over with.

She thought she'd be nervous. She was about an hour away from being a divorced woman and no longer a homeowner.

Two for one. This should be easy. Especially when she and Ashley didn't have anything to settle on. Ashley hadn't put anything down on the house. Hadn't even helped Marci choose a house. Hell, she hadn't even helped her house hunt. Not one dime had she put into Marci's new home, no matter how far Marci had had to travel to find it. The house was hers and hers alone. Had been from the minute she sat alone at the closing and then waited patiently for the next year for Ashley to move her belongings in.

From the minute Marci's feet touched Arizona dirt, she'd done all she could to prove to Ashley that she wanted a forever life with her. To provide for Ashley. What a mistake that had been.

But at least she'd get something back. Every dime of her money as the last bid had been exactly what she'd been looking for, even though she hadn't jumped fast enough, and after the Realtor contacted them they said they were still more than interested in buying the house and were ready to sign the papers immediately, with cash.

Marci couldn't get back the time or the heartbreak she'd put into Ashley, but she could damn well chalk the loss up to a lesson learned and a mistake she would never make again.

Never, ever again.

The secretary ended the phone call and the room was silent again. Her mind slipped to Tessa. To the last time she'd seen her. Those eyes. Watching her. Those sad eyes pleading with her to stop. To listen. To hear.

There was nothing to hear. She'd heard all she wanted to hear. Seen all she needed to see when Tessa protectively stepped in front of her slutty sister. How dare she take her side. How dare she.

With a huff, Marci raked her fingers through her hair and shifted in the chair, wishing her lawyer would hurry up with the paperwork so she could sign everything and get the hell out of this stuffy office.

She wanted out of this state. Out of this heat. Out of Ashley's life and her world forever.

The front door opened, and Marci glanced around to find Ashley stepping inside. Her pale blue eyes landed on Marci, and sadness filled them.

Marci had a flashback of the first time she'd ever laid eyes on her. Ashley had been decked out in snow gear after just ending a ski lesson, sitting in the coffee shop with her group of chattering friends, when Marci ducked inside to grab a hot chocolate before she headed home for the day.

As soon as Ashley had turned those eyes on her, Marci had felt the connection. Or rather, the inability to disconnect. Something in those eyes made her keep watching the group. And something in that smile and flirty eyes had encouraged her to introduce herself to the table of giggling women. To Ashley in particular.

Marci had been awestruck.

And then she'd become an idiot. She'd become obsessed with her, spending every available minute of Ashley's free time getting to know her. Then when it was time for Ashley's vacation to end, she'd ask if there was a possibility for a future. With those pouty lips pursed, Ashley had told her there was, but only if Marci was willing to move. There hadn't been a thought process for Marci. She was in. One hundred percent, she was all in. So she'd gone after her, followed her, and soon created a life with her.

And here she was, only feet away, looking just as good today as she had all those years ago. Wearing tight blue jeans with a pair of black pumps and matching deep vee blouse, she was still gorgeous.

But one thing was missing this time. Marci's heart. Ashley had ripped that out and stomped on it. She'd made sure Marci could never give it to another person.

Also, that flutter. That flutter was gone. That quickening in her gut, gone. That instant connection that had been all consuming so many years ago, was no longer present.

All gone.

Marci was suddenly grateful. For once, the sight of Ashley didn't weaken her knees. Didn't make her stomach knot and didn't make her heart skip.

As if mentally summoned by Marci's sudden discomfort, by the need to get the hell away from Ashley, to get on with the next phase of life, whatever that was, her lawyer stuck his head around the corner. "Marci. Ashley. We're ready. Can you join us in the conference room?"

Marci shoved out of her chair, eager, ready.

"Marci," Ashley softly said her name.

That sound used to drive Marci stupid.

This time, it irritated her as she turned to face her, taking in the sadness in Ashley's expression.

"Can we talk before we go in?" Ashley asked.

Marci turned to her lawyer, hoping he would deny the request. He gave a nod.

She turned back to Ashley. "Sure."

Ashley's led the way back out the door. Out into the sunshine. The heat. The devil's heat.

She walked halfway down the sidewalk before she stopped and turned to Marci. Sadness filled her eyes and she fidgeted with her hands, something Marci used to find adorable. She would do anything to make Ashley's worry go away, to make her forget. Now she just felt pity and had no desire to ease her worry.

Ashley had done an awful thing, got caught, and was living with the consequences. Sure, Marci could forgive her. But to forgive, she would need to forget. Forgetting was impossible. What Ashley had done, Marci could never forget.

"I've wanted to talk to you so bad." Ashley looked down at the ground then slowly back up at Marci. "To say how sorry I was for what I did."

Marci studied her pretty eyes and didn't see anything but regret in them. Good. She deserved to see regret. Ashley owed her that much.

Ashley shifted uncomfortably while Marci remained silent. But inside, she was hearing Tessa. Hearing Tessa's words. Her promise.

You're going to run across her again someday. Ask her why. Your closure will be in her answer. I promise.

Was she right? Would the closure be in Ashley's answer? Did Marci even want to know why anymore? What would it change? Nothing. It wouldn't change anything. But the answer didn't need to change to get the answer. Isn't that what Tessa had said? That she deserved to hear that answer?

Before Marci could change her own mind, before the voices could talk her out of asking the question, Marci gathered her courage and let the words out. "Why, Ashley? Why did you do it?" She shoved her hands in her pockets to keep from crossing them protectively across her chest.

Ashley closed the distance, her eyes suddenly full of hope. "I felt so abandoned, Marci. I was always so alone. You were working all the time and constantly talking about starting that stupid business in that dreadful cold place. Not to mention you always had Wendy in your ear talking shit about me." She squeezed Marci's arms. "I thought I was losing you. I thought Wendy was going to convince you to go back home. I freaked out, Marci. I did a horrible, lousy thing. Could you ever find it in your heart to forgive me?"

With every word, Marci felt more anger gathering.

Was Ashley serious?

Coming from a woman who did girls' night out every weekend with her besties while Marci worked overtime to learn how to be a travel agent. She didn't have time to be lonely. Coming from a woman who didn't mind entertaining their friends while her wife was selling another vacation package to replace the money Ashley had spent on day spas. Again, no time to be lonely. And coming from a woman who had picked up a woman during one of those girls' nights out then carried her home, to their home, and fucked her in the very bed they'd picked out together with the commission from those sales during those overtime hours.

Tessa was right. God, how right she was. The closure was definitely in the answer. And it was so damn loud.

And then something else Tessa said blossomed in her mind.

She wasn't your team player. She doused your flame.

She should have bulldozed you to the finish line.

Damn if Tessa wasn't right again.

Ashley hadn't been her team player. Her equal. Her ride or die. And she'd allowed Ashley to douse her flames for what could have been an amazing future. She could have had an amazing life had a piece of ass not caught her attention. If she hadn't been too weak to walk away. If she hadn't been smitten with the beautiful Ashley.

Marci felt the door of closure slam as Ashley looked up at her with those pleading eyes, waiting for her response, waiting for Marci to say something.

No. She was waiting for Marci to cave. To cave to those pretty eyes. To those full, pouty lips. To her pathetic excuses. She expected Marci to succumb to her because Ashley had known the secret all along.

That Marci was her puppet.

Oh, how good it felt to feel those strings snap one at a time.

How amazing it felt to know, to feel, that Ashley hadn't won after all. She hadn't gotten the last laugh. She hadn't broken Marci after all.

Ashley squeezed her arms again and pressed her body against Marci, dragging a single finger along her arms. "I know you miss me. I miss you so bad. And I miss us. Will you please forgive me and then take me home? Please, baby?"

Marci stared down at her for several long moments, waiting for the right words to surface, for the correct response to lead the way. Surely those words were in there somewhere. She'd spent eleven years with this woman. Eleven years worshipping her. There had to be something she needed to say.

"Say something, Marci."

Marci suddenly knew exactly what she wanted to say.

Nothing.

She wanted to say absolutely nothing.

Well, maybe there was one thing.

Marci chuckled. "You're so fucking pathetic."

She backed away, shook her head in disgust, and walked back into the lawyer's office.

Thirty minutes later, with her head held high, she walked out a divorced woman and her house sold.

Nothing had ever felt so good.

Well, maybe there was one thing that felt better. The realization that she'd treated Tessa so wrong. That she'd said some horrible things to her. To Monty. That she now knew Tessa was right about one thing.

It wasn't Monty's fault.

And she couldn't wait to get back home to tell her how wrong she'd been.

If Tessa would listen.

If she would accept her apology.

If she would allow Marci to give one.

CHAPTER FIFTEEN

I need two of those heaters on either side of the altar," Tessa instructed Gary, the guy from the rental company who had been amazing and patient with her all day. "Center them on the outside so the palm trees will hide everything."

"Yes, ma'am." He eagerly rushed away.

The poor guy had been running all morning. Moving heaters, waiting for Tessa's approval, then moving them again when she wasn't happy with the results, all with a smile on his face like he was happy just to be helping. Maybe he was just happy to be part of something that could be epic if it turned out to be identical to the photo in her mind.

Everything had to be perfect. This was it. The final hoorah. The end shebang. The wedding that would either make her a winner or send her home in tears.

The couple who would be walking down this aisle in just a few hours had to be over the moon excited about what Tessa had created for their first wedding. A first wedding for both of them. Thank God.

Tessa was more thrilled about that. That neither had been married before. She wasn't sure she could have put this much love and attention into a second or third marriage. Sure, she would have forced herself to do the job, because her future depended on it, but her heart wouldn't have been in it like it was for these adorable people.

Their video had been even more precious. Holding hands through their entire interview. Staring over at each other like they couldn't let the other out of their eyesight. She, Harley, wanted a beach wedding so she could walk barefoot in the sand. He, Robert, wanted a mountain wedding so they could be snowed in on their honeymoon and he could be the person to teach her how to ski.

She and her team had mulled over different ideas, tossed a few plans around, but only one scenario took hold for Tessa, and she knew she wouldn't be happy with anything less than exactly what they wanted.

A beach wedding. A mountain wedding.

There was only one choice for Tessa.

She decided to give them both.

So she brought the beach to the mountain.

Seven truckloads of beach, to be exact.

That decision had been the first time Seth had questioned her motives. The first time Danny had actually spoken an objection. And the first time Sally had been silenced. And she couldn't forget Monty's cocked brow, silently telling her she'd lost her mind.

"What in the world would we do with all of that sand after the wedding? It's not like we can sweep seven tons of beach under the couch." Seth chuckled nervously.

"There's a playground behind the resort. There's another playground in town at the park. There's an elementary school. I'm sure they could use some fresh sand. And the high school has an outdoor volleyball court as well as the community center. We can share it with everyone. I'll make the calls to make sure we can disperse it to anyone willing to take it." Tessa tapped her pen against the table and scanned the expressions staring back at her. They all looked so serious. Didn't they believe in her? Hadn't she proven herself already? "Next issue?"

"What about all of those palm trees?" Danny glanced down at the sketch Hunter had drawn as Tessa detailed the layout. "Like, all hundred of them according to this cool artwork."

"This resort is huge and could use some upgraded greenery. The new resort will be twice this size. Wendy said she would be more than happy to disperse the dwarf palms throughout both facilities. And I've contacted a tree expert who specializes in recycling palms. He is going to take them all. All ten of them, Mr. Overdramatic."

"And this wall of succulents?" Sally finally found her voice. "Where in the world would you put a seven-foot-high wall of plants?"

"The lodge." Tessa quickly added. She'd already envisioned the perfect spot for them. "The indoor Jacuzzi with that incredible view. Catty-corner them on either side of the sliding doors. Won't obstruct that panoramic scenery at all. Not to mention, the walls are already bare and need some decoration. The plants will love all that heat and steam. Wendy already approved that as well."

"Is there anything you haven't thought of?" Seth asked, pure admiration in his voice.

"Isn't that my job? To think of everything?" Tessa blew him a kiss.

"I'm in." Sally laid her arm across the table and formed a fist. "Let's do the damn thing!"

"Team Tessa!" One by one, everyone fist-bumped, and Tessa knew they were all on board with her insane plans to bring a beach to a snow-topped mountain.

With a sigh, she looked over her creation and felt the excitement curl tight in her belly.

Rows of white chairs, draped in Mediterranean blue, dominated the sandy grounds. Tropical foliage lined both sides like a paradise. With an archway draped in live plants, all tucked into the lattice to create a wall of nature, completing the scene.

Tall propane heaters were masked by the foliage to give the beach heat, and the altar had been set against the cliff to overlook the peaks and valleys blanketed in snow beneath.

For sure, she'd outdone herself and given her clients exactly what they wanted. And then some.

Even these final changes they were making, nothing more than minor alterations, hadn't bent her out of shape or caused her to second-guess herself.

There was no way in hell the other crew could outdo this magical creation.

Of that, she was positive.

"I have six more boxes of taffeta for the archway," Seth announced excitedly. "When your guy gets done with the heaters, we'll get that started."

Tessa nodded as she took in the whole scene. The ripples in the sand that created a perfect beach replica.

"I'm so amazed with us," Tessa confessed under her breath.

"You know you're going to win this thing, don't you?"

"We." Tessa turned to look at him. He had become her friend, a guy she hoped to always stay in contact with. Her crew had been more than she could have ever hoped for. "*We're* going to win this thing. Now get away from me before I roll out my bottom lip and ruin everyone's day."

He gave her a timid smile and cocked his head. "You are adored." He scurried off before Tessa could smack him, or cry. Right now, with so much beauty transforming around her, with the win only hours away, she could sink into this sand on her knees and just bawl her head off.

This whole journey had been incredible. Even the Marci drama was worth the hassle to be standing right here, right now, witnessing her victory unfolding before her very eyes.

"Tessa. I'm truly in shock right now."

Tessa turned around to find Wendy, eyes wide as she took in the surroundings.

"Thank you. I'm kind of taking it all in myself."

Taking in more than this scene was what she was doing. Taking in the fact that Marci was a coward. That she'd run off like a scorned brat without so much as an explanation. That she hadn't even bothered to say good-bye. Or answer her phone calls or texts, which Tessa had finally stopped.

Coward. Marci was a twisted, butthurt, blame everyone else for my sorrows, coward. Tessa should count her blessings that it was all over.

"Whatever in God's name made you think of this?"

Tessa shrugged. "My mom always told me to give your customers what they want. Times five."

"That is one smart mom you have."

Tessa grinned. "That she is."

She was truly blessed to have such an awesome mother who didn't buckle under the weight of the world. Who stood tall and faced defeat like a damn boss. Who smiled at the woman who could have been blamed for tearing her marriage apart. Who, instead, treated that mistress with respect and kept it moving.

She did that for her daughters. She knew they were watching. Knew they would learn from her behavior.

Oh, how Tessa had learned. If only Marci could learn the same lesson. If only Marci could get that damn closure so she could eventually move on with her own life.

If only.

But for Tessa, the sky was about to be her limit.

She could go anywhere. Any state. Maybe even another cold, snow-covered mountain.

But one fact was crystal clear. She couldn't stay here.

This was Marci's home. Her best friend. Her resort and her world.

Tessa didn't belong in it.

When the silence and Wendy's approving inspection got too much for Tessa, she couldn't hold back the question any longer.

"How is she?"

Wendy turned to look at her but didn't immediately answer.

Tessa knew this situation was hard on Wendy, but she wouldn't retract the question.

She wanted the answer. If only that one answer. Sure, she had more questions. Like where did she go? Was she coming back? Had she raced back to Arizona to forgive a cheater?

Actually, she didn't want those other answers. She just wanted to know that Marci was okay.

Wendy moved closer and lowered her voice. "I'm stepping out of boss mode and into friend mode because I shouldn't talk about her, but I don't want you to worry. She's fine."

Tessa didn't feel any better hearing that she was fine. Actually, that made the other questions rush to the surface.

"I'm glad to hear that," Tessa lied.

She was still mad. Pissed that Marci had left without so much as a good-bye. Without talking to her. Without a damn thing.

She just left like Tessa didn't matter.

Because, truth be told, with all of Marci's actions speaking far louder than her words, Tessa didn't matter.

She'd done what Tessa hadn't been able to do.

Walk away.

"She went back to Arizona to close on the house and sign her divorce papers," Wendy added. "And she decided not to come back until the contest is over." She fidgeted with the zipper on her jacket. "I'm sorry, Tessa."

Tessa felt the quickening in her gut with Wendy's confession.

To sign her divorce papers.

She'd found the courage. For that, Tessa was proud. She deserved the freedom to move on. Even if the steps only took her to the privacy of an office or a cabin where she couldn't be bothered by human contact.

"Please don't be sorry. None of this is your fault. Just be glad you don't have a slut for a sister." Tessa added a laugh, but it didn't reach her heart long enough to give off a joking feeling.

Screw Marci. Just fucking screw her.

She was a coward and Tessa didn't have any more time to devote to cowards.

"I'm actually glad you stopped by. I was going to come talk to you." Tessa could hear the quiver in her voice.

"Don't you dare say it, Tessa."

Tessa watched as Gary wheeled the last heater to the opposite side of the altar. "You know I can't work here if I win this thing. And I have every intention of being the winner."

Wendy didn't respond and the silence grew, but Tessa refused to look over at her. She didn't want to see pity or sorrow or even anger in Wendy's eyes. Her best friend was part of that decision. That had to make Wendy feel partially responsible. And Tessa couldn't blame her. She would do the same thing. Had done the same thing. And she would do it all over again.

She just wanted to move on. This win would surely bring more offers than this amazing resort. Even if this resort was the only place Tessa wanted to be. Where she envisioned working for the rest of her life.

"We have another resort in the Bahamas. I'll be more than happy to ship Marci there so I can keep you here with me."

Tessa finally turned to look at her. Wendy's brow was arched in a serious yet playful expression. Tessa laughed. Soon, Wendy was laughing with her.

It lifted the burden off her shoulders for some reason, and Tessa knew no matter what, everything was going to be okay.

So what if Monty was a player? She was single and could do anything she damn well pleased.

It was the married women in this world who needed to get their acts together and remember why they got married in the first place. They were the ones who needed to be loyal.

"What are you two cackling about over here?" Monty walked around the front of them and gave Wendy a flirty smile. The one that normally had women flocking to her side. Then again, most of them flocked long before she had a chance to notice them.

It was gross and Tessa resisted the urge to roll her eyes.

Monty was always going to be Monty, and one day someone was going to stop her in her tracks. Then and only then would she change her playing ways.

She couldn't wait for that day to come.

And with the way these two were staring at each other, like the rest of the world had just gone up in a puff of smoke, she wasn't too sure Monty wasn't already meeting her match.

"Hello, Monty," Wendy purred and turned to Tessa, back in boss mode, dismissing Monty entirely. Tessa had the impulse to hug the hell out of her. "As for your decision, we never had this conversation. I don't want you to make a rash decision. Sleep on it. And depending on tonight's outcome, we can talk more about it. Okay?"

"Deal."

Wendy glanced back to Monty and let her gaze flick down her body. "Good-bye, Monty."

She turned and walked away while Monty watched her retreating steps.

"I'm going to marry that woman," Monty whispered.

"In your dreams." Tessa grabbed her arm and turned her in a circle. "Now get your ass back to work. We have a contest to win."

Monty started walking. "And you're going to be our wedding planner."

"Shut up, twerp."

Monty tossed her a snarl over her shoulder before she headed to the altar to join Seth and Danny.

The mocking nickname made her think of Marci again.

She was ending her marriage while Tessa created one for someone else.

The fact was sad as much as it made her happy.

She prayed Marci found the closure she had no idea she hadn't found yet.

Maybe the next person in line would get the real Marci. The Marci she was sure still existed somewhere. Her heart tugged a little with the thought. She hadn't been the one Marci needed to tear down her walls. She hadn't been the person to turn Marci's world bright once again.

And that was okay. One day, someone special would come along for Marci, and then all of the pieces would fall back into place.

And it was okay that Tessa wasn't that person.

So she lifted her chin and dove back into work.

Soon, a bride was going to walk down this aisle. Down her beach on this mountain.

Because Tessa was awesome like that.

And soon, she was going to get to share that awesomeness with the whole world.

CHAPTER SIXTEEN

Marci snuck into Wendy's office and dropped into the chair across from her desk.

Wendy looked from the computer to Marci and arched a brow. "What the hell are you doing here? You said you were staying in Arizona another night."

"Hi, Marci. How was your flight? Did the weather suck? Did you sign those damn divorce papers? Did you kill that bitch?"

Wendy's expression softened. "Sorry. I'm…" She waved her hand. "Tell me! Tell me everything. It's done, right? Like, signed on the dotted line and that bitch is history, done?"

Marci gave a firm nod. "Yes. It's done. She is history."

Wendy jiggled in her chair. "It's not normal to be this happy, is it?"

"Probably not."

"I'm going straight to hell and I think I'm okay with it."

Marci chuckled.

Wendy composed herself. "So how are you with everything?"

Marci considered her next words. To be honest, she hadn't expected to feel so good about an ending. But she did. She felt great. "I'm fantastic, actually. It was the best feeling in the world to cut her cheating ass loose."

Wendy snagged her reading glasses off the tip of her nose and pushed her hands toward the ceiling. "A-to-the-hell-to-the-men! Hallelujah! Praise God. Hail Mary. Head, heart, shoulder, shoulder. All that holy good shit. I'm so freaking happy right now I could scream!"

Marci chuckled. "Don't go overboard. Your computer might self-destruct or something."

Wendy looked back at Marci and lowered her hands to her lap. "I think I see my best friend in those eyes again."

"I think I can feel your best friend in here again." Marci shrugged. "That happens when you give someone five minutes to explain why they stabbed you in the back."

"You did not!" Wendy snapped her glasses against the desktop. "You know she's a lying sleaze. You can't trust a damn thing that comes out of her mouth."

"I needed to hear her answer."

"What the hell for? So she can blame you? Isn't that what cheaters always do? Turn into victims when they get caught?"

That's exactly what Ashley had done. She'd blamed Marci. Blamed her for starting a new career and leaving her dreams in the snow. Blamed Marci for trying to make a great life for them no matter how hard she'd tried to keep their romance alive with surprises and gifts. She'd blamed everyone but herself.

Exactly what Marci had done.

Marci let Tessa's face bloom in her mind. She'd asked that question for Tessa. Because Tessa promised she would find her closure.

Damn, had she ever found it. Ashley had called her dream stupid. Blamed Wendy for getting in her head. Ashley had deflected the question in every way possible.

Every door had slammed shut with every word that spilled off her lips and then the revelation, the ties that had bound her, had begun to unravel. She'd seen Ashley for exactly the person Wendy had seen all along. Seen her crystal clear.

And even though she didn't hate Ashley, she didn't like her at all. Not anymore.

"Closure."

"Um-hmm. And did you find it?"

"Absolutely."

"Oh my God. You're actually smiling. I haven't seen that particular facial expression in years."

"Don't exaggerate. It hasn't been years."

Wendy dismissed her with a wave of her glasses. "Whatever you say, buttercup."

Was Wendy right? Had it been that long since she was actually happy? Yes. Maybe it had been. Obviously she'd been blind this whole time. Obviously only the outside world could see that she was drowning in her own hell.

And that world, and that hell, was over now. That place and time was in her past. In her rearview mirror. Exactly where it belonged.

As immature as it was to wish for such a thing, she hoped karma found Ashley one day. She hoped someone Ashley loved with everything she had inside her, broke her heart in the exact same way. Then and only then would she understand the magnitude of her actions.

But at the same time, Marci felt free. Light. Reborn.

Instead of being petty, she should be thankful.

Maybe one day she would be.

For now, that door was closed. That past gone. And she was so ready to move on with the next step. Ready to make sure she lived every day making sure that the piece that Ashley got, the piece Marci thought she broke, wasn't the best piece she had to offer.

Thanks to Tessa, she knew there was life on the other side.

"What time is the wedding?" Marci couldn't wait to talk to Tessa.

Only a few more hours, and she could face her again. Ask for her forgiveness. Ask her if they could start new. Have a redo. And then see where this thing, this incredible, fun thing, could go.

She'd felt it all along. That grip of need. That seed of want. That thing inside every person that let them know they'd met someone special. That they didn't want to be without them.

Tessa had made her feel that thing again and she didn't want to lose her hold on it.

"Three hours. I've visited both sites and I must say, this is going to be one hell of a finale." Wendy perched the glasses on her head. "But what Tessa did still blows my mind. Her imagination is priceless. She brought the damn beach to the mountain."

"The beach?"

"Yes. The beach. The bride wanted a beach wedding. The groom wanted a mountain wedding. So Tessa called every landscape company within a hundred-mile radius until she found someone willing to haul the sand to her."

"Impressive. Doesn't surprise me though. She's not a take no for an answer kind of girl."

"Impressive isn't the half of it. She turned the whole space into a tropical forest with heaters and beautiful decorations. Every species of succulent plant is on the mountaintop right now. It's the most beautiful, thoughtful wedding I've ever seen anyone plan."

"She's a pretty thoughtful person," Marci admitted. And sexy. And demanding. And sexy when she was being demanding.

What would it hurt to go find her now? To hell with waiting until after the contest was over. She wanted to see her now. Wanted to kiss her now. Wanted to drop to her knees and earn forgiveness. Right now.

It was insane how crazy she was about that feisty little fireball. How ridiculous she'd been all along. From the very beginning. If only she hadn't been closed to the subject. Closed off to finding love again. To commitment. If only she hadn't blamed Tessa's sister for Ashley's wrongdoings. If only she hadn't been such an asshole.

"Very thoughtful. But I need to tell you something," Wendy said.

Marci felt the punch coming but couldn't prepare herself for it. Not today. Not when so much weight had been lifted from her shoulders. Not when she had a mission of making her wrongs right again.

"Good or bad? Please don't tell me anything bad today. I'm happy and I even smiled for you."

"She's decided not to accept the position at the resort, even if she wins."

"Damn, Wendy. All you had to say was it's very bad." Marci raked her fingers through her hair and sighed. "Fuck. It's because of me."

"No doubt. Can you blame her? You were a complete jerk."

"Let me go talk to her. I can change her mind."

Wendy shook her head. "Not a chance in hell. You stay away from her until all of this is over. If she wins, you can work your magic and talk her into staying. Or at least try. I'm actually super bummed about it. But what she doesn't know, she has emails already pouring in. I have at least twenty-three solid offers from very reputable venues and resorts asking for her. I may have screwed up by doing the weekly televised interviews and pasting pictures into the blog and website. Maybe I should have kept this little contest all to myself instead of looking out for some of the losing teams. I don't want to lose her to any of them."

"Tonight. I'll talk to her tonight. I'll change her mind." Marci hoped.

Wendy was right. No good would come of her getting in the middle of a wedding that Tessa and her crew had worked hard on this week. Her final round in this competition. She didn't need any added stress to an already heated competition.

With a sigh, Wendy leaned against the desk. "Now that you're back to the old Marci, have you taken a good look around? Notice anything? Recognize anything?"

"Notice what? Just spit it out. You keep hinting, and obviously I'm missing something super important."

Wendy watched her for several seconds, those eyes drilling into Marci, then she put her glasses back in place and turned her attention back to the computer. "Just let me know when you do. In the meantime, you need to go grab an empty room and get cleaned up. You look like shit. And stay the hell away from Tessa until this thing is all over. I mean that."

Marci wanted to push her on the mystery, on what she was missing, but Wendy wouldn't budge. She knew Wendy well enough to know that. She would hold out until Marci saw it for herself. Which sucked because obviously Marci was missing something pivotal.

"So cheerful you are." Marci pushed out of the chair. "How did I ever survive without your whip?"

"You didn't. That's why you dragged your ass back up the mountain."

"Smartass."

"And don't you forget it."

❖

Tessa and Danny stood at the back of the rows of chairs, opposite of Seth and Sally, watching in fascination as their bride, Harley, stepped through the curtain and took in her surroundings for the very first time.

Her expressions transformed from curiosity to complete shock to utter amazement. Tears welled in her eyes and her hand flew to her mouth.

That look, that stunned expression of adoration, was the only thing Tessa needed to see to know that she'd done the right thing. She'd gone outside the box and made the unthinkable a reality for that very expression. She didn't need to win to know she'd just made Harley the happiest girl on earth. She'd given her a dream wedding. That was priceless.

Harley took her daddy's arm and started down the aisle. The smile on her face was contagious, and the love on Robert's face at the end of the aisle was adorable.

They were so in love, and every person witnessing such a precious union was blessed to be in their presence. And they all knew they were blessed.

Tessa didn't know what it felt like to be a mother, wasn't sure she ever wanted to know, but she had a sneaky suspicion it was something super close to the warm and fuzzy emotion snaking all through her body right now. She'd never been more proud of planning a wedding than she did for these two.

They were perfect and their love was like a beacon of hope.

It truly existed. This can't live without you love.

Tessa could barely contain her gushing delight. This wedding was her baby. Their baby. That was their bride. Their groom. From the sand that the landscape companies swore couldn't be delivered, to the tropical oasis even her crew thought was questionable, this was their seed finally blooming into a magnificent flower.

Harley spotted Tessa and mouthed, "Thank you."

Tessa gave her a quick wink while she fought back the tears.

Danny wrapped his arm around Tessa's shoulders and drew her close. "You just became her hero," he whispered.

Tessa let her head fall to his shoulders and nodded, too choked up to respond, and watched Harley continue walking toward her beaming groom.

Everything was so beautiful. Not just the surroundings. Not that she had given them both exactly what they had wanted. Not that she had gone far outside the comfort zone of safe. But that she'd done it for two people who truly deserved it. For two people who were so in love everyone around them felt it too.

They reached the end of the aisle, and her daddy bent down and placed a kiss against her cheek then moved to sit besides his wife, Harley's mother.

Harley turned to Robert, a look of pure adoration on her face, and joined him in front of the archway.

She looked stunning in her sleeveless off-white Bohemian style gown that ended just below her knees. The tattered edges drifted around her legs with the light breeze tricking every eye around them into believing they were on a beach somewhere, that the heat around them was from a sun beaming down on them. Her head was adorned with a flower crown with trails of ribbon dangling down her back. And her feet were entwined with crocheted toe sandals that wrapped around her ankles.

Tessa thought of her own life. Would she ever fall in love? Would she ever get a wedding? Did she even want one or would she be content without all the fuss? If she ever fell hard for someone, would they love her with every ounce of their being?

Thoughts of Marci bled into her mind. She'd struggled over the past few days to keep her out. Demanded she stay out. She wanted Marci gone. For good and forever. She didn't want to think about her. Didn't want to want her. And she sure as hell didn't want to miss her.

But she did. Dammit. She missed her. Missed the easy way they had connected. And the makeup sex. She very much missed that.

But more than those traits, she missed their common denominator. Their love for nature and the instant attraction that had bound them both together.

More important, she missed not knowing what could have come next for them. She shouldn't wonder. At all. Marci was too unsteady. She wasn't secure on her feet. Didn't trust. Maybe she didn't want to open up ever again. Maybe love wasn't in her future.

And why did Tessa care? She wasn't looking for love either. God knew, she'd had enough of spreading her magic over marriages she felt were doomed from the beginning. Hated wasting her time for people who'd already done the rodeo once or twice before.

So what if Marci didn't want a forever after? So what if she wanted to fuck her way through the rest of her life? So what?

But the so what was the part that nagged at Tessa the most.

She cared about that so what.

Dammit. She did.

For the first time in her life, she cared about someone else's desire to never feel love again. She wanted Marci to find that closure. She wanted her to see that she'd simply been with the wrong one the whole time. And that was okay.

Fuck. It was. It was okay. Maybe it took more than once or twice or even three times for people to find their perfect fit. Their perfect person.

Had she been blind all of these years? A hypocrite through every second wedding? A bitch with every third?

God. She had. She was willing to tell Marci to dust off her knees and get back on the horse. Why wasn't she willing to be happy for those who did just that? Who got back on the horse. Who went out and found happiness. Who believed they had found their person and went for it.

And why was she suddenly coming to this realization?

Because she missed sex?

No. She couldn't be that shallow. Sex was all around her. In every bar. Every nightclub. Hell, she could find sex online.

So why couldn't she shake this one? Why couldn't she shake Marci? And how was she supposed to move on wondering what could have come next for them? Why was it a constant hum in her mind? That next step.

That next step was love.

Warmth spread over her as the word echoed in her mind.

Yes. It was love.

She had felt it all along.

She'd been fooling herself from the second Marci accused her of cheating. Even earlier. When she'd scanned her surroundings in a room of flashing strobe lights and found Marci staring back at her. Then. She'd even felt it then.

What an idiot she'd been. Thinking that what they had would end with the ringing of the contest bell. Thinking that win or lose, it meant their finale as well.

It hadn't meant that. It could have gone further. Could have reached further. Of that, she was sure.

What they'd found in each other couldn't have ended there. She was a fool to believe otherwise.

In just a few short weeks, she'd tripped and fallen flat on her face in love. Yes. She'd done that. The unthinkable. The unimaginable. She'd done it. Fallen in love. That thing she didn't believe possible for herself. Love. She'd felt love. Still felt it. That feeling was in every thought of Marci. Every memory. Every flash of their time spent together.

It was love.

And now it was all gone. In the blink of an eye, that glimpse of hope, that flutter of emotional attachment that she'd never experienced before, had vanished.

Tessa would never get to know if Marci found her closure. If she found her answers. If she could ever open her heart again.

It made her sad. For Marci, she'd like to know that she'd moved on and found happiness. That she'd gone after that dream. If her ride or die pushed her to grab it. If she helped her grab it.

Marci deserved that. And Tessa wished only the best for her.

But the fact remained. Marci was gone. She'd skipped out like a coward. She'd blamed the wrong people. And now she was gone.

Maybe one day she'd run across Marci again.

She'd ask her why. Why had she left. Why had she done it without saying good-bye.

Maybe Tessa would get her own closure in the answer.

CHAPTER SEVENTEEN

Tessa stared at the plate of food in front of her. A beautiful filet mignon and loaded baked potato that normally would have been devoured within minutes of the waitress setting the meal in front of her.

Not this time. Her stomach was knotted tight, too tight to force food into the mix. The longer she stared, the more her stomach twisted.

She was going to hurl if that phone didn't hurry and ring.

It had been two hours since the bride had stepped out from behind the covered gazebo to find a tropical world all around her.

Her expression, that awed amazement, with those tears that followed, was what drove Tessa to bust down the walls of the box. Especially for those experiencing love and devotion and commitment for the very first time. Although a little eye opening had convinced her that she might have been wrong about that all along.

But if that fucking phone didn't hurry and ring to let her know if she had been hailed the winner, she was going to combust.

Her crew was steady chattering among themselves, laughing out loud, having a great time, acting as though that phone call didn't matter a bit.

"I'm going to steal that phone if you don't eat," Monty said, drawing Tessa out of her deep thoughts.

"Why haven't they called?" Tessa pushed the plate away with a huff. "Wendy should have called by now. Something's wrong. I can feel it."

"Stop it!" Seth blurted from across the table, his own steak half gone. "The phone isn't going to ring because Wendy is going to walk through that door any second to announce to all of us that we won the damn thing!"

"Hell yes!" The crew cheered and fisted their hands in the air then chanted, "Winners! Winners! Winners!"

Loving affection spread all over Tessa and the tension loosened its hold. She was truly blessed with these incredible people. From her last-minute changes, to her over-the-top ideas, they had stuck by her side and just let the flow carry them. She was so thankful for them and knew the only way to repay them for their unwavering support was to get that damn phone call. From there, their futures were limitless. They would get incredible offers, win or lose, and could go anywhere they wanted. Knowing that made her so happy.

The phone shrilled and the table went deathly quiet.

Tessa looked over at Monty, all of a sudden unable to move.

"Answer the damn thing!" Monty said.

Tessa slowly picked up the phone and turned it over to see Wendy's name in the ID box.

Her heart stumbled. "It's her!"

Unable to sit with so much adrenaline pumping, Tessa hit the connect button, then she tapped the speaker button, and stood.

"Hi, Wendy. I have you on speakerphone. The whole crew is here."

"Hi. Tessa."

Tessa sat back down with Wendy's monotone voice.

It was over. They had lost. She could read the answer in the sound of Wendy's tone.

She hadn't been good enough. Had gone too far outside the box. Maybe not far enough outside of it.

Whatever reason that made them fail, she only had herself to blame. The crew had followed her every command. Her every wish. Done exactly as she said. This was all her fault.

Tessa shoved out of her chair again. "We're on the edge of our seats, Wendy. Just say it."

Monty leaned toward the phone. "She speaks for herself. The rest of us are enjoying a delicious meal. Want to come join us?"

Wendy giggled lightheartedly while Tessa gave Monty a death stare.

"Maybe another time," Wendy added.

"I'm holding you to the date." Monty leaned back before Tessa could knock her back.

"Tell me, Wendy. I'm dying." Tessa debated sitting again.

Wendy took in a deep breath, and Tessa could hear chatter and movement through the phone. People talking nearby. The unmistakable sound of cars passing by. A light breeze against the mic.

"Before I give out the scores, I need to let you know that for this last leg of the race, we secretly added two people into the scoring process. One was picked from each of your delivery crews as well as a personal family member who would be close enough to oversee the entire transformation. In your case, Harley's father was that secret person as well as the man who delivered and set up your heaters."

Seth smacked the table. "That would explain why her daddy followed us around all day. And here I thought he just adored my company."

Everyone gave a quick laugh but soon turned their attention back to the phone in Tessa's grasp.

There was more movement on the line. Another car. More people talking.

"With those two people, the other team had a total score of seven hundred seventy-four points."

Tessa's heart sank. That was a pretty hefty score. Far higher than she wanted. Than she expected. Each member of the team, all five of them, could collect a perfect score, which was unlikely, but would they get higher than that?

Her heart stumbled, and she glanced down at Monty then slowly sank into the chair again.

Tessa stood up again, unable to control herself, terrified the final answer would buckle her knees. "Okay."

"Your two extra scores, Harley's dad and your delivery person, came to a total of one-hundred ninety-six."

"Awesome!" Hunter yelled.

Everyone leaned in to fist-bump her while Tessa stood frozen, anxious for that final score, her stomach tied in knots once again. She was positive she could feel her face flushing and her ears ringing.

"Your personal crew scored…"

Tessa sank to the chair once again, terrified of the answer, terrified they had lost, more terrified that she was going to faint before Wendy revealed that score. Monty leaned into her as if she could feel Tessa's tension. The room was so quiet. She could hear her own heart thundering against her ears.

"Five hundred…"

Tessa was holding her breath. Her lungs burned. Her head swam.

Monty tightened her grip.

"…ninety-three…"

Joyous cheers erupted around her, and Tessa had to let the number sink in, trying to do the math in case their outburst was short-lived.

Five hundred ninety-three plus one hundred ninety-four.

"Stop doing the math! You won!" Monty yanked her out of the chair. "You won, Tess!"

Tessa burst into happy tears.

She dropped the phone on the table as Monty wrapped her in a hug. Before she knew it, the entire crew was draped over her, all hugging and crying and squealing.

They'd done it. All of it. From the crazy friends that wrecked the lodge, to the insane boxer's party in the middle, to this last perfect, extravagant wedding. They'd won the damn thing and their lives were going to drastically change because of their hard work.

Everything about their worlds was going to spin out of control. They were going to move on to bigger and better things. They were going to be known all over the airwaves. Their hometowns would name a landmark after them.

Of course, she was going a little too far with her wild imagination. They weren't celebrities, after all. But right now, the sky felt like it had no limits. For any of them.

Well, except for Tessa. Her future was still up in the air. Her change was still yet to be determined. She'd spent this entire contest, knowing this resort, this mountain, and this world, was where she was going to spend the rest of her life. Where she had dreamed of spending the rest of her life.

Now, she had no clue. That decision, where to go, what options were available, was still unclear and that made her uneasy.

She didn't know what the future held for her. She'd worked so hard for this win, to be able to stay right where she was, and now she couldn't. It wasn't fair that everything had been yanked out from under her. It just wasn't fair.

But dammit, they had won! They had beaten seven other teams and were standing here now victorious. That meant everything. That paled in comparison to where she would end up. Where they all would end up. And she couldn't be more excited no matter how confused about that future she was.

Finally, everyone moved back to their chairs, wiping cheeks and sniffling, happily chatting and full of excitement.

"We never doubted you for a second, Tessa!" Sally raised her glass of wine. "To Tessa. The fiercest leader and teacher and friend I could have ever hoped to work with. I am amazed at your talent. And your balls."

"Hear, hear!" Danny chimed in.

Seth clinked his glass then stood. "And let's not forget that she told off a two-hundred-pound drunk boxer with nothing more than a whisper."

"Hear, hear…" They all began to chime again.

Monty jerked her glass back. "What the—wait! What boxer?"

"Camille Jenkins!" Seth blurted. "Big, tough badass, wall of knockout trophies 'cause she knocks people the fuck out, Camille Jenkins!"

Monty turned back to Tessa with a wide-eyed expression. "I don't think I want to know."

Tessa laughed. "Good. Because I don't want to retell it."

She lifted her glass to the center. "To all of you. The best crew I could have ever dreamed of having. Together, we kicked this thing in the ass!"

Glasses clinked again and everyone cheered. Tessa only wished she knew where her story would end. What state would she wind up in? Would it be cold? Would there be snow? Would it be a beautiful resort like this one?

Or maybe she'd wind up somewhere like home. Hot. Dry. Hot.

She was so tired of the heat.

Monty stood up so fast her chair slid several feet behind her.

Tessa turned to look up at her and found her blank face staring at the doorway.

Before she even looked, her heart knew. Before her eyes could see what would make Monty's expression be ripped from a smile to a frown, her soul could feel.

Chapter Eighteen

Marci gave a tight nod as Monty stood to full height behind Tessa's chair, her expression and posture indecisive as she stared across the room.

She'd seen that particular look once before. In her very own bedroom. While Ashley had scrambled to cover her naked flesh.

But not Monty. She'd simply watched Marci. Waited. Almost expecting a specific outcome.

Thinking back, had she wanted Marci to have that reaction? Had she wanted a bloodshed conclusion? Had she wanted Marci to charge at her?

It was a question Marci wasn't ready to ask. Might not ever be ready to ask. That night had been the end of her marriage. The end to the life as she had known it for so many years. Simply put, that night had been the end. And Monty was a part of that.

So no. She wasn't ready to fist-bump or shake hands or even be her friend. But one fact remained. To be in Tessa's life, if she would give Marci an undeserved second chance, Monty would be part of that world as well, and Marci was willing to figure out where they went from here.

Tessa adored her little sister. Loved her unconditionally. No matter her faults, no matter how her actions drove Tessa insane, she would always be blood bonded.

And Marci would have to accept that. Was ready to accept that.

Tessa turned to look up at her sister, but Monty never took her eyes off of Marci.

No doubt, Marci had left her no choice but to jump to the defense, to be on guard. She'd been a complete ass to Monty and Tessa. A ridiculous, non-trusting ass.

So much for first time impressions with her family.

She definitely had some amends to make.

But right now, Monty wasn't her concern. Tessa was.

Her amends had to start there.

Tessa slowly turned and locked Marci in her gaze. A smile threatened her lips and her eyes softened. Marci's breath hung in her chest while Tessa slowly pushed away from the table and stood. She was so beautiful with her tear-streaked face. Her eyes seemed greener than the last time she'd seen her.

Raw images flashed through her mind. On her knees in the pond house, working for Tessa's forgiveness. Their time behind the waterfall. In her bed. Her insides clenched tight while the Rolodex of images spun faster.

And then Tessa's expression morphed as if she suddenly remembered that she was mad at Marci. As if she finally recalled the fact that Marci had lost her mind and gone postal on her and her sister.

Yes. She'd done that. The embarrassment might forever haunt her.

Tessa's lips thinned into an angry line, and she said something to Monty before she started across the room.

Marci wanted to lift her chin in confidence. Fact was, she wasn't confident of anything anymore. She didn't deserve to lift her chin. If anything, she should hang her head for being such a complete idiot. For being so bruised. For taking it out on Tessa. For not trusting a woman who had never given Marci a reason not to.

Instead, Marci stood her ground, kept her eyes focused on Tessa, determined to take the tongue-lashing. To take whatever Tessa dished out. And then to beg her, if needed.

Tessa came to a stop directly in front of her. "What do you want, Marci?"

"Can we talk?"

"Talk?" Tessa shoved her hands on her hips and tilted her head back. "Don't you think it's a little too late for that?"

It was all Marci could do not to pull Tessa forward and clamp their lips together. This little feisty woman had shown her that there was life on the other side of death. That her bright days could carry on no matter how dark they had been. That she wasn't broken after all.

Now she felt whole again with all of her baggage left in Arizona. All she wanted was another chance to begin again. With Tessa.

"Is it?"

"Don't you dare deflect. You don't get to do that," Tessa spat through clenched teeth. "You walked away like a coward."

"I know."

Being so close to Marci was too much when all Tessa really wanted to do was kiss her. She wanted to circle her arms around her neck and lock her legs around that waist, then ride her until an orgasm made her forget that Marci had been a complete immature asshole.

How could she want anything to do with Marci right now?

She'd hurt her, as hard as that was to admit. In only eight weeks, Marci had managed to get to her. To that soft part of her. To her heart. And then she'd walked away as if Tessa didn't mean a damn thing to her.

Maybe because Tessa hadn't voiced that fact. That she felt anything at all.

But she did feel something. Oh, how she'd felt. Too much, in fact. So why hadn't she told Marci? Why hadn't she been brave enough to just say she was having fun, that she liked her, maybe more than liked, and that she'd like to keep doing just that. If only that.

And now she was pissed. And angry. And she would be damned if Marci got to deflect from the root of this malfunction.

Marci stepped into her. "Tessa, I'm so sorry."

Tessa angled her head. "Sorry for what, exactly?"

Marci tugged Tessa's hands off her hips. "I'm sorry that I acted like a jerk. That I blamed your sister. That I left without saying good-bye."

Tessa wanted to jerk her hands free of that soft embrace. No. That was a lie. She wanted that soft embrace all over her naked flesh. Inside her. Coaxing her to an orgasm. Oh, so bad.

Marci stepped even closer. "I'm sorry that it took me so long to find my closure. I'm sorry that the sight of your sister made me lose my cool. I'm sorry that I hurt you. More than everything, I'm sorry for that. I would never do anything to intentionally hurt you."

Tessa looked away. She hadn't expected Marci's apology to grab her heartstrings. She also hadn't expected to believe every word she was saying. She was too mad for her words to reach that deep. But dammit, they did. They were reaching all the way down to that hard center and melting her reserve.

Fuck. She didn't want to cave. Marci didn't deserve that just yet.

She needed Marci to work a little harder. From her knees would be a perfect position to earn forgiveness.

Marci let go of one of her hands and tucked a finger beneath Tessa's chin. She tilted Tessa's face up.

"Is it too late, Tessa?"

Tessa studied those beautiful brown eyes. She wanted so badly to lie right now. She desperately wanted to tell Marci that it was all over. Whatever it had been, that it had been shut down.

Truth was, she was more desperate to see what the next phase of this life held for her. And she wanted to do that with Marci. By her side. In her world.

God, she wanted that more than she wanted this win. More than she wanted that future.

More than anything, she just wanted Marci.

"No."

"Before I kiss you, I've been instructed to send you outside where Wendy and a gaggle of reporters and photographers and only God knows who else, are waiting for you."

Tessa could only nod, wanting nothing more than that kiss.

Marci bent down and pressed their lips together.

Cheers erupted behind them.

Time seemed to stand still while Tessa snuggled into Marci's arms.

Right. Marci just felt right. Like Tessa fit only in her grasp.

Excitement rolled through her as Marci tightened her grip and deepened the kiss, while everyone clapped behind her. This was her new beginning. And she couldn't wait to see what this new life had to offer.

Marci pulled back and Tessa immediately missed the pressure of those lips. Butterflies erupted in her stomach. Love. She was so in love that it made her emotional.

And she could see that love reflecting in Marci's eyes.

Dear Lord, she couldn't wait to see where this love carried them. She couldn't wait to explore this newfound thing. This thing that had such a hold on her that it frightened her as much as it excited her.

She just couldn't wait to take that next step.

"Marci!" Seth yelled from the table. "It was you! It all completely makes sense now!"

Curious, Tessa turned around to find Sally and Danny huddled around Seth's phone. Monty, however, was still standing in the same spot Tessa had left her, her expression blank, yet her shoulders were no longer stiff.

Who could blame her? She'd been the person who helped break up a marriage. Even if the fault didn't rest with her, her part in the drama had been played.

That part Tessa couldn't fix. What she could do was love them both until they figured out how to make up and move on.

"I'll make things right with your sister," Marci whispered and took Tessa's hand. "Soon. I promise."

Tessa looked up at her. "I'd like that. But not today. Let her worry for a minute longer. She deserves that much."

Marci grinned.

"Holy mother of all things perfect, we get to stay!" Seth said.

"What is he rambling about?" Marci asked as she squeezed Tessa's hand.

"We all get to stay!" Seth looked away from his phone and stabbed Tessa with wide, excited eyes. "Oh my God! We all got hired by the resort!" He started jumping up and down and was quickly joined by Sally and Danny. "We get to stay! We get to stay! We get to stay!"

Tessa pulled Marci with her and joined the trio. "Whatever are you talking about?"

Seth shoved his phone at her. "Hit the play button."

Tessa did as instructed. Wendy appeared on the screen. Her hair was drifting around her head with the breeze, and the sun was shining bright. Cars passed her by and Tessa recognized that she was outside the restaurant. A reporter was standing beside her, microphone in hand.

"So, Miss Highland, tell me where this winning crew goes from here."

"They go nowhere. They all stay right here, at this resort, which is what the contest was all about from the beginning. We needed to find a solid, proven crew that could handle the fundamentals of catering to an elite group of clients."

"And when you say elite, who or what are you referring to?" the reporter asked.

"The rich and famous. Stars. Celebrities. Clients who simply want their privacy. Who don't want the hassles of planning their vacations, who want someone to scale down the details and make their wishes reality, and are willing to pay a professional to handle everything and keep their identity secret."

"Did you have such clients for this contest?" the reporter continued.

"No. These clients were just ordinary, everyday vacationers who signed up via the resort website to be part of this contest. Free of charge. From the party animals, to brides, we encouraged everyone to apply with a video of what kind of vacation they were looking for. My brother and I went through every video and picked out each client based on easy to plan, to hard to handle. These contestants had a complete mix of good and bad, and it was up to each crew to give the clients what they wanted. We were looking for someone who wasn't afraid to go the extra mile."

The reporter moved the mic back. "Because you were looking for a crew you could trust with the real agenda? The elite clients, as you called them."

"That's exactly what I was looking for. And I found them."

Marci held her breath. Holy shit. That was *her* dream. *Her* plans. *Her* desire. The very one she'd tossed aside to be with Ashley. The very one Wendy had been hinting about this whole time. Asking her time and time again had she seen it yet.

How had she missed that? How had she not seen that everything happening around her, the crews, the clients, was parallel to the dream she had shared with Wendy? Right down to the nitty-gritty details. She was the only person Marci had ever shared the detailed information with before she got whisked away into fantasy land.

How the hell had she been so blind?

"And your resort is where this will all take place?"

“Absolutely. We’ve already escalated our building plans on the east side of the resort to include five brand new lodges. All private, non-connecting properties, all equipped with everything a mountain vacation should include, and each client will have their very own crew to see to their every need.”

“Sounds intriguing. Is there a possibility that a star, say a star like Lady Gaga, Ellen DeGeneres, or Angelina Jolie could be one of your elite clients vacationing at this resort in the near future?”

Wendy gave a shy grin and a shrug. “Who knows. Could be. But I’ll never tell.”

The reporter laughed. “Can you at least give me a hint?”

“I’ll just say that since the contest began, my inbox has grown with clients eager to get on that list. And now we have a top notch crew to put that company into motion and train more crews.”

“How are you going to take care of this amazing resort as well as a private company with so many clients?”

“Oh, it won’t be my burden to bear. That job, that new company, belongs to Marci Jones.”

Shocked, Tessa looked up at Marci and found an expression of pure disbelief.

“Marci gave us full control to select the clients and the contestants, and in return we got to piggyback off her dream with free advertisement. Win-win for everyone involved. All we had to do was use the resort as home base to find the perfect crew. And we gave them some really hard clients. Some very tough. And as you see, only the strong survived them all.”

“Tessa Dalton’s team?” the reporter asked.

Tessa threw her free hand over her mouth and Marci gave her a squeeze.

“Yes. Tessa’s team proved themselves weekly. And their finale was a phenomenal, miles outside the box, brilliant performance. What she did for her bride and groom took her to another level of planning. It was incredible, actually. We knew she and her team were the ones for the job when we saw what they had put together." Wendy looked directly at the camera, and Marci knew that look was for her.

It said, "Do you see it now? Do you see what I've been doing for you?"

She had the best friend in the whole wide world. God knew she didn't deserve her.

Marci mentally choked back her tears. Wendy had done that for her. She'd taken her notes, her detailed notes, and turned them all into reality, all while Marci moped and bitched and fell deeper into her own despair.

How ever was she going to repay such a carefree act of love?

EPILOGUE

Tessa stepped through the front door of the mountaintop lodge. She stalled to look back over the snow-covered grounds, at the peaks and valleys in the distance, and resisted the urge to hug herself. This was her favorite place in the whole world. In the whole wide world. Where she felt at home. Where she felt free and protected at the same time.

It was just a house. Huge, of course, but it was still just a home. But something about this place just took over her emotions every time she stepped inside.

She spent as much time in this beautiful house as possible. From setting up for clients to just hanging out when the place was empty. She couldn't get enough of being there.

A whole year had passed her by since she'd won the contest. Since Marci had asked for a second chance.

In that time, she'd covered thirty plus weddings at the resort and planned several large group events, all while watching the construction of the new lodges being built. Like this one, they were huge and fancy and amazing. But for some reason, they still held no candle to this one. They didn't make her feel connected like she did with this one.

But the most important thing she did feel connected to was Marci. Inside. Outside. In bed. Out of it. Every fiber of being was connected to that woman.

And now they were connected through Marci's business. Their business.

Zen.

Tessa had to hold back a squeal as she turned to close the door.

She'd done that. Won a contest. Become the shit in the wedding world. And in that time, she'd helped Marci roll the contest over into a business. A thriving business.

Wendy had brought her dreams back to life. How incredible was that? How much love would a person need to do that for their best friend?

But she had. She brought Marci's dreams back to life. The very ones she'd allowed Ashley to make her forget.

And together, Tessa and Marci had taken on their new clients. Six of them, to date. Prestigious, rich, secret clients. And Marci had seen to it that they paid a beautiful price to get the best private treatment.

Their every command had been met. Sometimes before they even had time to command it. Yes. Their crew was that good. With Seth, Danny, Sally, and Hunter leading every step of the way.

There was no better crew for the job. And Seth was the perfect leader. He was even given that title and that responsibility by the entire crew. And he was fantastic at that job. He had an eye for detail and like Tessa, went above and beyond what the clients wanted or needed. And with the three amigos as his sidekicks, there was no client who could ever want or need for anything.

Tessa wanted to pinch herself sometimes to make sure she wasn't dreaming. That she was still alive and not in some purgatory space between heaven and earth.

Life was so good. So good, in fact, she often worried that it was all too good to be true. Nothing could be this incredible and stay this perfect forever. Yet, so far, it had. It was perfect. Her life. Love. Everything. Absolutely perfect.

And to add the cherry to her mountain of whipped delight, Monty had found her match in life. Wendy. Of all people, Wendy.

She'd never seen Monty crushing on anyone. Let alone in love with someone. But damn, she wore it well. Nor did she know her little sister, who'd spent most of her life kicked back while women flocked to her, had done all of the chasing to catch Wendy's eye. She'd wined her. Dined her. Went completely out of her normal way to catch her.

It had taken Marci some time to open up to Monty, but once she did, all was forgiven. Or at least driven to the back of her mind where it was safe to actually care about Monty. They opted to never speak about it again, and that was good enough for Tessa. She wasn't sure she could have continued a relationship with Marci otherwise. Positive she shouldn't have, in fact. She loved her sister, was in love with Marci, but having two of the people she loved the most in this world at odds with each other would have been too much. It would have been her doom. Her and Marci's doom.

And having Monty on this mountain with her was amazing. Of course, Michelle was jealous at times, claiming Tessa loved Monty more than her. But when she'd come for a visit several months back, she'd actually hugged their little sister and told her that she was proud of her accomplishments, but mainly she was proud that she'd settled down.

The shocked expression on Monty's face had been worth all the years of distance between them. Michelle had made her day, year, maybe even her life, with those simple few words.

Tessa's life couldn't get any fuller. She was filled to the max with blessings and never missed a day to thank her lucky stars. Or to blow kisses to those mountaintops.

She turned toward the large open room to find rose petals and tea light candles scattered across the floor, trailing toward the staircase that led to the upper floor.

With a wicked grin, she dropped her bag of cleaning supplies on the table by the door and started walking. She shed her coat and shoes, wondering if she should be stripping her clothes with every step, praying Marci would take care of that little task when she finally found her, no doubt, in that ridiculously huge master bedroom.

Damn, her heart was so full. Full of Marci. Full of happiness. Full of a great life. Just full.

She'd never been so in love. Over the moon, couldn't get enough of her, in love. Every day she wanted to spend with this incredible woman. Because every day was a new adventure. Every day was another great thing to explore. Together.

It was crazy how deep she'd fallen. Crazy how she couldn't get enough. Insane how she never wanted to get enough. But scary at the same time. Scary that at any second, the rug could be ripped out from under her feet. It would send her spinning out of control. That she knew.

Marci had done that. Marci had made her feel that secure. That Tessa could trust her with her life, with her soul, with her heart. So she did. Everything within herself, she gave to Marci. Openly. Unendingly. Without question or hesitation, she gave it all to Marci.

With her heart pounding with excitement, Tessa started up the staircase and listened for any sounds of Marci.

All was silent as she took yet another step.

Halfway up, she found a piece of paper with a single word.

You.

This was so Marci. She was always surprising Tessa with fun, sexy adventures. Always making her feel special. Loved. Adored.

Another few steps, she found another note.

Like.

Unsure if she should be naked when she finally found Marci, hoping Marci would command her to get naked very soon, Tessa took the final steps to the landing and found yet another note.

Me.

Tessa quickened her steps. The next note was only a few feet away.

Best.

Again, Tessa scurried down the hall until she found the next.

On.

Tessa snickered. She knew exactly what the final words would say. Her favorite position for Marci. On her knees. Good God Almighty, but the magic she could work from that position.

Another few steps took her to the bedroom door, where she found the final note on the floor.

My knees.

For sure, she should have been stripping with every step.

With her insides tight, Tessa opened the bedroom door to find Marci down on one knee with her hands behind her back.

Her breath jammed in her throat while her heart overflowed.

Love. She was so in love with her. She wanted to spend the rest of her life doing exactly this. Following rose petals and sexual notes. Making love and experiencing incredible new adventures. On this very mountain.

Marci gave her a bright smile.

Tessa took two timid steps, terrified her knees would buckle and send her sprawling like a damsel.

Was this it? How Marci would propose to her? On bended knee? The exact position she'd told Marci was lame when they'd ventured into the conversation of marriage a few times. It was a subject they didn't speak of often.

Not because Tessa didn't want to marry Marci one day. She did. Very much. But Marci had already been down that road. Had already had her lavish wedding. And that marriage had crashed and burned, and she'd made it clear very early in their relationship that she had no intentions of doing it again.

So Tessa had avoided that talk. Avoided her true feelings on the matter. Instead, she'd implied that proposals were overrated. That if or when someone ever proposed to her, it better not be that customary position.

And watching Marci right now, down on that one knee, she hadn't meant a damn word. This was exactly how she saw her own proposal. And right now, it was perfect.

Marci was perfect.

"Tessa?"

Tessa couldn't breathe. Her heart was beating so fast she had a moment of fear that this would be the last thing she ever saw. Marci down on bended knee.

Marci pushed out a piece of paper that resembled a contract and held up a pen. "Will you buy this house with me?"

Tessa burst out laughing, but regret washed over her soul. She'd thought that was it. The moment. Her time.

"Wait. *This* house?"

"Yes, ma'am. This house. With me. Will you buy this house with me?"

Tessa flew across the room and sank to her knees in front of Marci. She flung her arms around Marci's neck and kissed her cheeks, nose, lips, neck, so happy she could barely think.

"Is that a yes?" Marci asked.

"Yes! Yes! You know I'll buy this house with you!"

"Great. But first..." Marci pulled the pen in front of Tessa's face and opened her fingers.

A diamond ring dropped down from a string.

"I really need you to marry me."

Tessa sucked in a startled gasp. Hot tears sprang to her eyes as she covered her mouth with her hand.

"And I don't want to hear a single complaint about this being my second go-round on this marriage thing."

Tessa stared down at that glimmering circle of silver bling.

The one that would bind them forever. The only one she ever wanted to slide on her finger.

A sob left Tessa's lips as she looked back up to Marci.

"Say yes, Tessa. Out loud."

Tessa let out a half laugh, half sob and flung herself into Marci's arms.

"Yes!"

About the Author

Larkin Rose lives in a blink-and-you've-missed-it town in the beautiful state of South Carolina with her partner, Rose (hence the pen name), along with a portion of their seven brats, a chunky grandson, and too many animals to name. Her writing career began years ago when the voices in her head wouldn't stop their constant chatter. After ruling out multiple personalities and hitting the keyboard, a writer was born.

Books Available from Bold Strokes Books

All She Wants by Larkin Rose. Marci Jones and Tessa Dalton get more than they bargained for when their plans for a one-night stand turn into an opportunity for love. (978-1-63555-476-2)

Beautiful Accidents by Erin Zak. Stevie Adams and Bernadette Thompson discover that sometimes the best things in life happen purely by accident. (978-1-63555-497-7)

Before Now by Joy Argento. Can Delany and Jade overcome the betrayal that spans the centuries to reignite a love that can't be broken? (978-1-63555-525-7)

Breathe by Cari Hunter. Paramedic Jemima Pardon's chronic bad luck seems to be improving when she meets police officer Rosie Jones. But they face a battle to survive before they can find love. (978-1-63555-523-3)

Double-Crossed by Ali Vali. Hired thief and killer Reed Gable finds something in her scope that will change her life forever when she gets a contract to end casino accountant Brinley Myers's life. (978-1-63555-302-4)

False Horizons by CJ Birch. Jordan and Ash struggle with different views on the alien agenda and must find their way back to each other before they're swallowed up by a centuries-old war. (978-1-63555-519-6)

Legacy by Charlotte Greene. When five women hike to a remote cabin deep inside a national park, unsettling events suggest that they should have stayed home. (978-1-63555-490-8)

Royal Street Reveillon by Greg Herren. Someone is killing the stars of a reality show, and it's up to Scotty Bradley and the boys to find out who. (978-1-63555-545-5)

Somewhere Along the Way by Kathleen Knowles. When Maxine Cooper moves to San Francisco during the summer of 1981, she learns that wherever you run, you cannot escape yourself. (978-1-63555-383-3)

Blood of the Pack by Jenny Frame. When Alpha of the Scottish pack Kenrick Wulver visits the Wolfgangs, she falls for Zaria Lupa, a wolf on the run. (978-1-63555-431-1)

Cause of Death by Sheri Lewis Wohl. Medical student Vi Akiak and K9 Search and Rescue officer Kate Renard must work together to find a killer before they end up the next targets. In the race for survival, they discover that love may be the biggest risk of all. (978-1-63555-441-0)

Chasing Sunset by Missouri Vaun. Hijinks and mishaps ensue as Iris and Finn set off on a road trip adventure, chasing the sunset, and falling in love along the way. (978-1-63555-454-0)

Double Down by MB Austin. When an unlikely friendship with Spanish pop star Erlea turns deeper, Celeste, in-house physician for the hotel hosting Erlea's show, has a choice to make—run or double down on love. (978-1-63555-423-6)

Party of Three by Sandy Lowe. Three friends are in for a wild night at billionaire heiress Eleanor McGregor's twenty-fifth birthday party. Love, lust, and doing the right thing, even when it hurts, turn the evening into one that will change their lives forever. (978-1-63555-246-1)

Sit. Stay. Love. by Karis Walsh. City girl Alana Brendt and country vet Tegan Evans both know they don't belong together. Only problem is, they're falling in love. (978-1-63555-439-7)

Where the Lies Hide by Renee Roman. As P.I. Camdyn Stark gets closer to solving the case, will her dark secrets and the lies she's buried jeopardize her future with the quietly beautiful Sarah Peters? (978-1-63555-371-0)

Beautiful Dreamer by Melissa Brayden. With love on the line, can Devyn Winters find it in her heart to stay in the small town of Dreamer's Bay, the one place she swore she'd never remain? (978-1-63555-305-5)

Create a Life to Love by Erin Zak. When sixteen-year-old Beth shows up at her birth mother's door, three lives will change forever. (978-1-63555-425-0)

Deadeye by Meredith Doench. Stranded while hunting the serial predator Deadeye, Special Agent Luce Hansen fights for survival while her lover, forensic pathologist Harper Bennett, hunts for clues to Hansen's disappearance along the killer's trail. (978-1-63555-253-9)

Death Takes a Bow by David S. Pederson. Alan Keys takes part in a local stage production, but when the leading man is murdered, his partner Detective Heath Barrington is thrust into the limelight to find the killer. (978-1-63555-472-4)

Endangered by Michelle Larkin. Shapeshifters Officer Aspen Wolfe and Dr. Tora Madigan fight their growing attraction as they work together to destroy a secret government agency that exterminates their kind. (978-1-63555-377-2)

Incognito by VK Powell. The only thing Evan Spears is focused on is capturing a fleeing murder suspect until wild card Frankie Strong is added to her team and causes chaos on and off the job. (978-1-63555-389-5)

Insult to Injury by Gun Brooke. After losing everything, Gail Owen withdraws to her old farmhouse and finds a destitute young woman, Romi Shepherd, living in a secret room. (978-1-63555-323-9)

Just One Moment by Dena Blake. If you were given the chance to have the love of your life back, could you ignore everything that went wrong and start over again? (978-1-63555-387-1)

Scene of the Crime by MJ Williamz. Cullen Mathew finds herself caught between the woman she thinks she loves but can no longer trust and a beautiful detective she can't stop thinking about who will stop at nothing to find the truth. (978-1-63555-405-2)

Accidental Prophet by Bud Gundy. Days after his grandmother dies, Drew Morten learns his true identity and finds himself racing against time to save civilization from the apocalypse. (978-1-63555-452-6)

Daughter of No One by Sam Ledel. When their worlds are threatened, a princess and a village outcast must overcome their differences and embrace a budding attraction if they want to survive. (978-1-63555-427-4)

Fear of Falling by Georgia Beers. Singer Sophie James is ready to shake up her career, but her new manager, the gorgeous Dana Landon, has other ideas. (978-1-63555-443-4)

In Case You Forgot by Fredrick Smith and Chaz Lamar. Zaire and Kenny, two newly single, Black, queer, and socially aware men, start again—in love, career, and life—in the West Hollywood neighborhood of LA. (978-1-63555-493-9)

Playing with Fire by Lesley Davis. When Takira Lathan and Dante Groves meet at Takira's restaurant, love may find its way onto the menu. (978-1-63555-433-5)

Practice Makes Perfect by Carsen Taite. Meet law school friends Campbell, Abby, and Grace, law partners at Austin's premier boutique legal firm for young, hip entrepreneurs. Legal Affairs: one law firm, three best friends, three chances to fall in love. (978-1-63555-357-4)

The Last Seduction by Ronica Black. When you allow true love to elude you once and you desperately regret it, are you brave enough to grab it when it comes around again? (978-1-63555-211-9)

Wavering Convictions by Erin Dutton. After a traumatic event, Maggie has vowed to regain her strength and independence. So how can Ally be both the woman who makes her feel safe and a constant reminder of the person who took her security away? (978-1-63555-403-8)

A Bird of Sorrow by Shea Godfrey. As Darrius and her lover, Princess Jessa, gather their strength for the coming war, a mysterious spell will reveal the truth of an ancient love. (978-1-63555-009-2)

All the Worlds Between Us by Morgan Lee Miller. High school senior Quinn Hughes discovers that a broken friendship is actually a door propped open for an unexpected romance. (978-1-63555-457-1)

An Intimate Deception by CJ Birch. Flynn County Sheriff Elle Ashley has spent her adult life atoning for her wild youth, but when she finds her ex, Jessie, murdered two weeks before the small town's biggest social event, she comes face-to-face with her past and all her well-kept secrets. (978-1-63555-417-5)

Cash and the Sorority Girl by Ashley Bartlett. Cash Braddock doesn't want to deal with morality, drugs, or people. Unfortunately, she's going to have to. (978-1-63555-310-9)

Counting for Thunder by Phillip Irwin Cooper. A struggling actor returns to the Deep South to manage a family crisis, finds love, and ultimately his own voice as his mother is regaining hers for possibly the last time. (978-1-63555-450-2)

Falling by Kris Bryant. Falling in love isn't part of the plan, but will Shaylie Beck put her heart first and stick around, or tell the damaging truth? (978-1-63555-373-4)

Secrets in a Small Town by Nicole Stiling. Deputy Chief Mackenzie Blake has one mission: find the person harassing Savannah Castillo and her daughter before they cause real harm. (978-1-63555-436-6)

Stormy Seas by Ali Vali. The high-octane follow-up to the best-selling action-romance, *Blue Skies*. (978-1-63555-299-7)

The Road to Madison by Elle Spencer. Can two women who fell in love as girls overcome the hurt caused by the father who tore them apart? (978-1-63555-421-2)